COWBOY'S TEMPTING NEIGHBOR

J.P. COMEAU

Ryan

"Hello, everyone! And welcome to another round of our barrel-racing bonanza! In fifteen minutes, our top-ten competitors, who have been whittled down all day, will compete for the top-five spots to advance to the state championship league. So, get your snacks, take your seats, and let the fun begin!"

I heard the announcer's voice off in the distance, and I drew in a deep breath. I rose to my feet from the metal bench I sat on, waiting for my name to be called. I was first up in the next competition, seeing as how my time beat out everyone else's today. And while confidence flowed through my veins, I wasn't a stranger to accidents.

"You've got this," I murmured to myself.

I opened my eyes just as the announcer stopped rattling

off advertisements, and I reached for my hat. I slid back my hair and tucked it beneath the brim, making sure it stayed out of my eyes. I had certain rituals before every race I participated in, some for luck and others for sanity. But, the one thing I never did was look in a mirror.

I pictured confidence on my face and forced myself to exude just that.

I reached for my locker and opened it up, taking stock of my boots down at the bottom. I stepped into my right boot before kicking out my left one, following a pattern I had derived for myself ever since I had started racing eight years ago. And after slipping into both of my boots, I loosened the flannel collar around my neck to give myself some breathing room before I turned toward the locker room door that slung itself open.

"I see you're still knee-deep in your rituals," Will said with a grin.

I chuckled. "Here to spy on me for Bryce?"

"What? Hell no. He kicked me out of his room thirty minutes ago."

I quirked an eyebrow. "So, what are you doing bothering me in mine?"

He grinned. "Wanted to come to wish you luck."

"Against your brother?"

He walked over to me and leaned in. "From one brother to another? We both know you're the better barrel-racer. You're going to wipe the floor with his ass."

I shook my head. "How much did you bet on me?"

Will stepped back, looking shocked. "Why, I never."

I barked with laughter. "That much, huh?"

He smiled brightly. "It's not much money, just enough to make things exciting."

"It better not be much, because otherwise Sadie's gonna have your ass for it."

"You know damn good and well I'd never put my family in jeopardy."

I snickered. "I'm just pullin' your chain, Will. I know you'd never risk them. But, if you win that bet, you owe me a steak dinner."

He held out his hand. "I'll get you a steak dinner every day for a solid week if I win this bet. How 'bout that?"

I shook his hand. "You got yourself a deal on that, brutha."

After dropping my hand, he winked at me and walked out of my private locker room, heading for what I assumed were the girls sitting in the stands somewhere. And briefly, I wondered if Ellie was around. I mean, I knew she'd be around professionally since she had this little arrangement of hers with Bryce and my other half-brothers. But, part of me wondered if she'd stick around personally, too.

Get your head in the game, Ryan. Eye on the prize.

"Five-minute call!" a man yelled as he walked down the hallway. "Five-minute call for racers one through three!"

I looked down at the number 1 taped to my chest. I felt it crinkling against my back, but I quickly blocked the sensation out of my mind. If I were going to get my weeks' worth of steak dinners, then I needed to whoop my half-brother's ass today. And that meant full concentration because Bryce was good at what he did.

Not that I'd ever tell him that shit.

I walked to the small outside window the locker room afforded me and gazed out over the stands. The sea of faces alone made me smile from ear to ear because I definitely enjoyed performing for a crowd. Adrenaline rushed through my veins. My heart started pumping as the seconds ticked by. People always came from all over central and eastern Texas to compete and watch these rodeos during the year. But today? It seemed like the entire state had crammed themselves into the stands.

Guess moving the family business to Conroe was a good thing, after all.

A knock sounded at my door, and I made my way out into the hallway. I needed to go find my horse and get mounted for my run. They'd determine the top five to progress today by taking the times from earlier and average it with the times we clocked during this race. So, I had to make sure that Mountain Dew and I were good and ready for this match—from how tight the saddle sat against his body to how locked in his metal shoes were.

Don't fail me now, Ellie.

I walked down the hallway, hearing my clicking boots echoing off the corners that surrounded me. I felt eyes on me, even though there was no one in the hallway, and as I rounded the corner, my back straightened. The last few minutes before any race were the most intense, and sometimes I got so excited that I actually grew erect. Weird, but it was all of that adrenaline coursing through my body and my heart pumping in my ears and the blood rushing at high speed through my veins.

There was something about it that couldn't be matched.

Not even with the most beautiful woman in the bed next to me.

"It's showtime," I murmured with a grin.

I emerged from the locker room and headed for the horse stalls. Clowns and referees entertained the crowd, shooting shirts at them and throwing water bottles for everyone to try to catch. The deafening roar blocked out anything in my mind that might've distracted me. And as I walked up to the stall Mountain Dew was in, a rodeo worker opened the metal gate for me.

"Need a hand?" he asked.

I shook my head. "Thanks, but I got it."

I placed my hand against my palomino. His cream-colored tail started swinging, and he shook his head, fluffing out his white main. The soft yellow of his fur gave way as my hand tickled against his side, all the way up until I grabbed the reins. Then, I slid my boot into the stirrup and hoisted myself up.

"All right, Monty. You ready, boy?" I asked.

I patted him softly against the side of his neck, and he bobbed his head. Almost as if he could understand me. And it made me chuckle.

"Then, let's go kick some ass."

There was nothing I wanted more than to find myself at this state championship rodeo being held in a couple of months. There was nothing I wanted more than advancing to that level and beating everyone out. If I could do that, it meant offers of advertisement and monetary support as far as my eye could see. And while I enjoyed the work I did with the petrol company, I wanted something that was my own. Something not attached to the family name that I could say I did of my own volition.

"First up, Ryan Remington! He's currently at the top of our leaderboard, so let's see if he can keep his lead! Ready, Ryan?"

I looked up at the announcer's box hanging high in the sky and gave him a thumbs up.

"The man's ready, everybody! Are you ready to see him ride?"

And when the crowd went wild, I felt the stampeding of their voices rattling my ribcage.

"Then, my friends, let the countdown begin!" the announcer exclaimed.

The ten-second countdown was always a haze. I closed my eyes and drew in deep breaths, centering myself as much as possible. I connected myself with Monty, a horse that needed no breaking in since he practically heeled to me the day he was born. He was my baby. My good ol' boy. The first horse that I had raised from birth until this very moment.

And when I opened my eyes, the bell sounded.

I perched on top of Monty as everything fell silent. I blocked out the sound of the bell and the cheers. I blocked out the squeaking of the rickety gate as it flew open. I even blocked out the sound of Monty's hooves pounding against the ground. All I focused on was the first barrel. It was less than twenty feet ahead of us, and I poised myself for the first turn.

Before I tugged Monty's reins to the left.

He took the turn so sharply that I felt the energy of the stadium through the ground my horse pounded upon. I was upright in a flash, heading for the second barrel that Monty prepared for even before I tugged my reins to the right. A smile flew across my face as his muscle memory kicked in. I pulled back on the reins, giving him the freedom to do what I knew he could do best. And by the time I rounded the last barrel to make the venture back, he was in complete control, while I was along for the ride.

Most riders yelled at their horses while they were racing. They would "yah" and "yeehaw" and all sorts of shit that was beyond unnecessary. I found that a horse raced the best when they didn't have so much to think about. So, I forced myself not to make a sound.

In and out, we weaved, kicking up dust and wrapping around barrels. Monty took some of the sharpest turns of any horse I'd ever been on, and it never ceased to amaze me as to how tired my thighs were as we came to the end of every race we had run together up until this point. But this time, things went differently.

This time, I felt something I'd never felt before.

"Monty!" I exclaimed.

I felt him falter, and I knew we were going down. As we

rounded the last barrel, his leg gave way before the sounds of the crowd came rushing back. I heard the thunder of their gasp. I heard people crying out in horror. Then, the last thing I remembered was being crushed against the ground with my horse on top of me and that last barrel rolling for my face as it tipped over.

2

Ellie

"*Hello, everyone! And welcome to another round of our barrel-racing bonanza! In fifteen minutes, our top-ten competitors, who have been whittled down all day, will compete for the top-five spots to advance to the state championship league. So, get your snacks, take your seats, and let the fun begin!*"

I drew in a deep breath and registered all of it as I stood beside my cousin, Sadie. I heard her two best friends cheering on the other side of her while Bart whistled wildly behind us. The smell of manure and fresh lemonade in the air reminded me of all the stuff I loved about a small town—things I didn't get back in Dallas.

I picked at the beds of my fingernails as I watched the massive clock on the light-up billboard count down. Throngs of people climbed over one another with hot dogs and dripping burgers in their hands as they tried to secure their seats for the next series of events. Today had been a long day, especially as a farrier for the Remington Brothers. But, they had been so generous to me since I had gotten into town, and I was more than willing to do the free work for what they were giving me in return—a chance to build my own blacksmithing business.

"Will! Up here!" Sadie exclaimed.

She flagged him down, and he started leaping up the steps. I watched in awe as Will practically lunged at my cousin, eager to kiss her like I wished my son's father would have been. Dallas was supposed to be the end of my journey. After my blacksmith and farrier training, I had been set to take over a small business in the area that my son's father had usurped because he had been so close to the family.

Then, I got pregnant, and my entire world came crashing down around me.

I wish I had someone like Will.

I was happy for my cousin, really. But, it was hard not to be jealous of her. She had always been so petite and kind. Mild-mannered and soft-spoken, and always turning the heads of men she never looked at. She was womanly and sensual and kind.

She was everything I wasn't, and sometimes it didn't shock me as to why I was still single.

Not that I needed someone. But, it killed me that my son didn't have anyone. His father had walked away from us when

I announced that I was pregnant, and the man I had fallen in love with evaporated right in front of my eyes as if he had never existed.

And when I called Sadie, crying about it, she invited me to come to stay with her and Will in Conroe until I could get my feet underneath me.

"First up, Ryan Remington! He's currently at the top of our leaderboard, so let's see if he can keep his streak going! Ready, Ryan?"

The announcer's voice pulled me out of my trance, and I peered down at the stables. I saw that massive, black, ten-gallon bucket hat he always wore that flew off every time he turned the first barrel with his horse. And when I saw him flash a thumbs up to the announcer's booth, I held my breath.

Come on, Monty. You've got this.

"The man's ready, everybody! Are you ready to see him ride?" the announcer exclaimed.

The crowd went wild, and a smile crept across my face. This was the kind of thing the guys were addicted to, and I understood completely. I had grown up around rodeos. They were the weekend entertainment in the small towns of Texas. But Conroe's rodeos had grown over the past couple of years to almost monumental proportions. And it brought a great deal of needed revenue to the small area.

"Then, my friends, let the countdown begin!" the announcer shouted.

I looked up and saw the ten-second countdown start. But, instead of keeping my eyes on the clock, they gravitated back to Ryan. I watched him focus, saw his back straighten. And right as the clock struck two seconds, he poised himself on his horse. There was an effortlessness to his movements that entranced me. There was an ease to his posture that kept my eyes glued to him.

But once the gate opened, the crowd went wild, pulling me, yet again, from my trance.

I do that a lot with him lately.

Sadie and the girls went crazy as they leaped to their feet. I stood and softly clapped, keeping my eyes trained on the horse's legs. I watched as Monty's hooves stamped into the dirt and sawdust. I watched as they took sharp turns around the barrels, making sure there was no faltering in Monty's movements that could be blamed on the shoes I tailor-made for their horses.

Then, it happened.

Every racer's—and farrier's—worst nightmare.

"Monty!" I yelped.

I saw the shoe before anything else. I watched it go flying into the air as if it had happened in slow motion before Ryan and Monty went down. I leaped over Sadie and her two friends in order to make my way toward the stairs. I lunged down them, two by two, scurrying toward the fenced boundary that blocked the crowd from the arena. In one fell swoop, I hopped it, booking it toward Monty as he crushed Ryan, trying to get up.

And after scooping the metal shoe off the ground, I raced to help get Monty off of Ryan.

"I've got Ryan up!" Willow yelled.

"I've got Monty, checking him out now!" I shouted. "It's okay, boy. Hey, hey, it's all right. Deep breaths. Calm down. There we go. It's gonna be okay." I patted his neck and tried to soothe him.

I peeked over the horse's back as the crowd collectively held their breath. I saw Luna trotting over to the referee, probably to get a deliberation on what they might do with Ryan's race. And when I looked down at the horseshoe in my hand, I tried to find any sign of what might have happened. Because before the race, the shoes were perfect. I would've staked my reputation on it.

"Ryan! Hey! You okay?" Bryce asked as he rushed up.

"Dude! What the hell just happened?" Bart asked as he skidded to a stop.

Then, Luna came rushing over. "Since Monty passed his tests before the race, the refs are taking some time to check the field. Especially since everyone saw his shoe go flying."

Ryan's voice caught my attention. "Any reason why that would have happened in the middle of a race?"

I tossed him the shoe. "Inspect it yourself. It's solid and intact."

I felt all eyes on me as the once-rambunctious crowd went dead silent. It felt like I was walking around in another universe or some shit like that. Ryan started stalking away from me as the referee came in our direction, and I couldn't help but register the stoic face he plastered on for the crowd. Ryan stood tall and strong like he hadn't just eaten sawdust in front of everyone, probably for the first time in his career.

I'm done for if this is my fault.

I knew he was trying not to look like an idiot in front of the crowd, and I wanted to do something to make this better. But, I kept my mouth shut. I knew where I stood with the brothers and with this arrangement, and I knew damn good and well that I couldn't screw it up, either.

My son, Micah, needed me to not screw this up.

When Ryan turned away from the referee, though, there was a grin on his face. A light in his eyes. And as he slid his hat back onto his head, our eyes met. I heard the announcer's voice come on over the intercom, but the world faded into the background as Ryan walked up to me with a swagger and a confidence that left me breathless.

Why did this man always leave me without a voice?

3

Ryan

"*After clearing Ryan and Monty of any injuries, the referees have determined that the cause of the flying horseshoe was related to an unauthorized wet patch of ground on the field. Once the problem has been contained, Ryan will be afforded another shot at his race. Let's give it up for the refs!*"

As I made my way for Ellie, I had half a mind to take her into my arms and plant a kiss right on that sexy, pouty lower lip of hers. With her wild and wavy blond hair blowing in the summer breeze and her deep, sea-blue eyes watching my every move, I felt more powerful than ever before. She did that to me whenever her gaze locked with my own. I rolled my shoulders back and felt my grin spreading across my cheeks. The smattering of freckles against her nose and cheeks glowed brightly as her skin tinted with the faintest blush.

And there was so much adrenaline surging through my body that I felt my cock capitalizing on the moment. I got to Ellie's side and quickly turned around. "We should really come up with a horseshoe that works when wet."

She snickered. "Good luck when waterproof plastic starts splintering and lodging itself into your horse's hooves."

"I take it it's already been tried?"

I saw her nod out of my peripheral. "Mhm, about a decade ago. Permanently maimed the horse, and they've been outlawed ever since."

I quirked an eyebrow. "That's an actual law?"

She shrugged. "Among farriers, it is."

Willow walked up to me with Monty. "I'm going to go reset Monty myself. Ellie? You want to come with me and get a fresh shoe on him?"

Ellie nodded. "Might as well change all of them to give him a fighting chance. Those shoes take a pounding with something like this. Ryan?"

I tipped my hat to her. "Go do whatcha gotta do. I'll be over at the stables."

Will patted my shoulder before escorting me back into my locker room, and it was there I splashed some water onto my face. I cursed beneath my breath as my cock finally started dwindling, and I gave myself a good, long look in the mirror. I saw the water dripping off my skin. I saw the panic behind my eyes that hadn't quite settled.

Then, Will appeared behind me in the reflection. "Monty's already been checked out. He's good."

I drew in a deep breath. "We sure about that?"

"Look, I know you're attached to this horse, and rightfully so, but Mountain Dew is just as strong as you are. It's not just owners who take after their animals, you know."

I chuckled as I reached for a towel. "Yeah, I guess you're right."

Then, Bryce burst into the room. "Ellie's got Monty's shoes fixed. They're all brand new, they're on a bit tighter, and everyone's ready for you."

I turned to face him. "I appreciate it, thanks, guys."

He looked at me quizzically. "You sure you're good enough to go back out there? You had Monty's full weight on your legs there for a while."

I shrugged. "Might as well race while adrenaline and shock still have me captive."

Bryce blinked. "You know that's not healthy, right?"

Will patted my shoulder. "Listen, if you're actually hurt—"

I shook my head. "Want me to take off my pants so you can see for yourself?"

Bryce smirked. "I mean, if you're into that sort of thing."

Will cackled. "If you like that kind of shit, go search Porn-Tube. But, I have no want or wish to see my half-brother in any sort of state of undress."

I smiled brightly. "Since when did our Will get so grown and proper on us?"

Bryce patted his back. "Since he got together with Sadie and kept getting in trouble for always embarrassing her."

Will groaned. "I just like sex, guys, and she knows I do."

I barked with laughter. "Better you than me, bud. Better you than me."

But as I started for the door, Will called after me. "When you get a chance, will ya let Ellie know it isn't her fault?"

I peered over my shoulder. "I'm sure she already knows that. Especially with the ref's ruling."

"Just say it to her anyway? She's always so damn hard on herself."

I nodded. "You got it, brutha."

As Will walked me back down the hallway toward the stables, I puffed out my cheeks with a sigh. I had one more chance at this race, and I didn't need to be blowing it because I was too distracted with how Ellie felt. I could speak with her after the race for as long as she wanted to talk with me. But, right now? I had to get my head back in the game.

I felt my palms sweating as I approached Monty. I put my foot into the stirrup and hoisted myself up, making sure I didn't hear him grunt or groan or anything of the sort. Sweat trickled down the nape of my neck as I wrapped my right hand up in the reins, my eyes trained on the newly sawdusted arena in front of me.

The ten-second countdown began, and I went through my ritual before I poised myself at the two-second mark.

Then, the gate opened.

"Yah!" I bellowed.

Everything went silent once more as Monty and I hurdled toward the first barrel. I crouched down, trying to make myself as aerodynamic as possible while I tugged Monty's reins to the left. We soared around the first barrel, and I pulled right quickly to get around the second one. Then, I felt Monty get his feet beneath him and take control of the field.

So, I loosened the reins and let myself go along for the ride.

It was over in the blink of an eye, and when the crowd went wild, I turned Monty toward the scoreboard. I read the time over and over again, trying to make sense of it. Trying to make sure I wasn't actually hallucinating.

"My God, he's done it! Ryan Remington beat his own best score by one and a half seconds!"

I dared anyone to beat me out of that time.

Monty and I trotted out of the arena as a grin slid across my cheeks. My heart soared with delight, and my cock stiffened with the adrenaline-laced happiness coursing through my veins. I felt unstoppable. I was on top of the world. And as I slid off of Monty's back so the stable hands could take him to be washed down and pampered, I set my sights on finding Ellie. I needed to thank her for her quick work.

"Hey, anyone seen Ellie? She's got a two-year-old son with her, name's Micah? Anyone seen a female farrier? Blond hair, blue eyes? Stands about this tall?"

Luna's voice sounded behind me. "Ryan!"

I whipped around. "Hey! Luna!"

She thumbed over her shoulder. "Wanna come sit in the stands with us?"

I jogged up to her. "Ellie up there with y'all?"

She furrowed her brow. "No, she left after you and Monty finished your race."

"Wait, she's not here anymore? Why?"

She shrugged. "Beats me. Micah was getting pretty fussy up in the VIP box, though."

I nodded slowly. "All right, well, yeah, sure. I can join y'all up in the stands."

"Everything okay?"

I'll have to send her a gift basket or something. "No, no. Just wanted to let Ellie know that what happened to Monty wasn't her fault."

Luna smiled. "Bah, she already knows that. The ref practically made that ruling on the spot."

"Yeah, well, you know how her mind is sometimes."

She blinked. "I mean, do *you* know how her mind is sometimes?"

I slipped off my hat and ran my fingers through my sweaty hair. "Anyway, yeah. Let me get a dog and some lemonade, and I'll come find y'all."

She pointed off in the distance. "Great! We're right up there in the section behind the last barrel, ten rows up."

I followed the point of her finger. "Sweet. I'll be there in a few."

And just as Luna walked away, I felt a strong hand come down onto my shoulder.

COWBOY'S TEMPTING NEIGHBOR

COWBOY'S TEMPTING NEIGHBOR

COWBOY'S TEMPTING NEIGHBOR

COWBOY'S TEMPTING NEIGHBOR

"Here I am, trying to find you to celebrate," Bryce said as he rounded around to my front, "and you're off questioning people on where Ellie is? I figured you would've already been in your locker room, throwing back some celebratory whiskey!"

I shrugged. "Yeah, well, I wanted Ellie to know all that shit wasn't her fault."

"Or, maybe you feel guilty about needing a second run because you didn't see the wet spot in time."

I grinned. "Or, maybe you're simply jealous that you're never going to be at the top of the leaderboard so long as I'm competing against you."

He clutched his heart. "Your words. They sting so much, Ryan."

I snickered. "Will some lemonade help heal that wound? Because I'm about to snag some myself along with a fully smothered hot dog."

He opened his mouth to take in a comically deep breath. "*Maybe* after my race so that I'm not puking all over Daredevil."

I stared, walking backward. "Suit yourself! See you up in the stands, brutha."

But in the back of my mind, I wished I would have caught Ellie before she had to head home. If anything, to thank her for the quick work she did getting Monty prepared for the second race.

4

Ellie

I jumped to my feet and cupped my hands over my mouth as Ryan cleared his second race. I didn't even have to look at the clock to know he had out-bested himself. I'd never seen a barrel racer book it the way those two just did, and as my voice rose above the chorus of clapping, people began whistling alongside me.

"Woo-oo-oo-oo-oo-oo!"

I clapped my hands so hard that I felt them burning. The thunderous roar that rose up from the ten thousand people packed into the stadium took my breath away. They drowned out my sound just as quickly as it had spawned, and when I saw Ryan trot off the field with Monty, pride filled my chest.

That's how you do it, boys.

Sadie tapped my shoulder. "It's for you."

I looked over at her before she put her phone in my face, and I saw she had a text message from her nanny, who was up in one of the VIP boxes with the kids.

Nanny: Let Ellie know that Micah won't go to sleep. He's been crying for a while now, and I'm not sure he'll make it through these last few races.

I leaned into Sadie's ear. "I'm going to go get him and take him home."

She hugged my neck. "Sounds like it's for the best. I'll bring you some dinner back from wherever we celebrate."

I kissed her cheek. "Thanks, Sades."

I pushed my way through the crowd and found the steps leading up to the VIP box Bryce had rented out for the kiddos so they could be with us today. I rushed up the stairs, taking them two by two before my son's sobs hit my ears. Oh, man, he sounded tired. His little two-year-old cry was nothing more than a hoarse whimper, and it made me wonder how long he'd been like this before the nanny had broken down.

"Miss Ellie, I am so sorry. I'm usually so good with—"

I cupped her cheek. "It's okay, I swear. I'm shocked he hung on this long. We've been here practically all day."

Micah whimpered, "Mommy, go home now?"

I scooped my son into my arms. "Yes, that's right. You and I are going home to cuddle. How's that sound?"

He buried his tired, wet face into the crook of my neck, and it broke my heart. I reached my free arm out to Miss Weatherford, the woman who had been so kind as to agree to help me with Micah while I was living in the guesthouse. She kept apologizing for "her fault" in Micah's mood, and I did my best to soothe away her fears.

After all, it wasn't her fault that Micah wasn't in bed already.

As much as I wanted to stick around and congratulate Ryan, though, I was ready to head home as well. Today had been filled with triumph, pain, fear, and chaos, and I was ready to close my eyes myself. Navigating through the packed crowd was enough to make even the strongest mother ornery, and by the time Micah and I got to my hatchback, he was already asleep on my shoulder.

"All right, let's get you home, little man," I whispered.

I kept peeking in my rearview mirror all the way home, watching my son while he snoozed. Part of me wanted to message Miss Weatherford and ask her when he'd last eaten, but I figured a big breakfast in the morning could remedy that. I didn't want to chance waking him up and pissing him off even more simply because I was a worrywart.

And maybe one day, Mommy won't have to work so many long hours.

I ran down my schedule for tomorrow in my head as we made our way back to Rocking R Ranch. I had a couple of possible client meetings that I didn't want to botch, and I had to finish up an order for a customer I had snagged last month that needed the iron railing on their second-floor balcony installed by this weekend. The pressure mounted with each client that came in, especially since I didn't want to let the Remington Brothers down.

But, I still had yet to secure a returning client, and I was growing worried.

Blacksmithing has always been a predominantly male job, and a lot of the prospective clients I'd met with throughout my career turned their nose up at my tits in the beginning. Usually, though, I'd had the man who would eventually become my son's father there to help offset whatever prejudice was going on in the client's mind. And I figured out very quickly that my downfall was selling myself.

Sure, I could sell my skills. For me to do that, though, I needed to build a portfolio. And that part of the equation had been a very slow grind. After having Micah and moving away from Dallas, I focused all of my attention on figuring out where I would plant myself so my son could have the best upbringing possible. So, it almost seemed like a no-brainer to come to Conroe, considering Sadie was the only shred of a family I had left.

Providing for Micah, however, was proving to be a more difficult task.

Over the past year or so that I'd been indulging in this agreement between myself and the Remington Brothers, I'd brought in more than my fair share of client inquiries. But, only about half of them converted to actual customers, and it took being burned six different times to set up the rule that if a job was commissioned, half of the job needed to be paid for upfront.

That didn't leave a lot of people left who were willing to take a chance on a female blacksmith with no portfolio, no degree, and no references.

It only took my ex bad-mouthing me once to a prospective client for me to get the picture with that one.

Still, I had faith in myself. I knew I could do this if I put my nose to the grindstone. And with the Remington Brothers fronting the cost of the equipment I needed and putting a roof over my head, it left me more time to worry about honing my skills and acquiring the customers I needed.

But again, it was a very slow process with many hard lessons along the way.

I enjoyed being their personal farrier, though. They treated their horses better than many other trainers did, and I had my own office. Not to mention, Bryce was letting me stay in his guesthouse until further notice with all bills paid if I didn't charge them for my costs as a full-time farrier. It was a dream, really. However, it wasn't the kind of dream I saw for myself and my son.

I wanted my own business to keep us afloat.

I wanted to purchase a home in my own name that my son could be proud of.

I wanted the kind of reputation Sadie had in her community.

And I no longer wanted to ride anyone's fucking coattails to get to where I wanted to be.

"Just keep working at it," I murmured to myself.

As I pulled into Rocking R Ranch, I heard Micah sniffling

in the back. I quickly parked and hopped out of the car, taking him into my arms before he fully woke up. I unlocked the door and walked him straight back to his room, where I carefully put him into bed. And as he turned away from me, pulling his favorite yellow blankie up to his chin, I drew in a deep breath.

"I'll do this for you, little man," I whispered.

I perched on the edge of his bed and stared off into a corner. The last two or three years of my life had been nothing but a whirlwind of disaster, chaos, and frenzy. One minute, I was training as a farrier and a blacksmith under one of the most capable men in Dallas, who also happened to be the man I loved. And the next minute, I was risking my own life to push out a son with an absent father who wrote me out of his life and gave me nowhere to turn.

I had to do this for us. I had to make blacksmithing work.

Because if I didn't, my son would have nothing.

And he deserved so much better than that.

$$\text{🙣} \quad 5 \quad \text{🙤}$$

Ryan
One Week Later

I straightened my tie one last time in the reflection of my truck before I turned toward the restaurant. I was about to meet with the man who had been kind enough to do it on our lunch break, and I had offered to pay. I had some sensitive information I wanted to discuss with him, and I knew he was the only man in my life who would understand exactly how I felt.

So, I started into the restaurant in my Gucci suit to find Dr. Valconie.

"Ryan! Hey!"

I entered the restaurant and turned at the sound of his voice. "Lance."

He grinned. "Come here, champ."

I chuckled as I clapped his back in a hug. "I take it you heard?"

He pulled back and squeezed my shoulders. "Everyone's heard. Congrats, man. How's the horse, though? I heard something about a shoe flying off or whatever? Did you have someone take a look at your leg?"

I snickered. "My leg's fine, a bit of bruising is all that happened. And Monty's great. Eating like a king right now and getting a bit of rest before we start up training again."

"So, you're heading back to Conroe soon?"

"This weekend, actually. I've got some work that needs to be taken care of in our new headquarters, and it'll keep me there until after the Texas Championship Rodeo."

He held his hand out. "Then, let's get to talking so we can set something in motion."

I quirked an eyebrow. "You act like you already know what this is about."

He chuckled. "Let's just say you're not as cryptic in your emails as you think."

"Oh, boy."

We walked through a series of aisles peppered with booths and tables before our hostess ushered us into a private room. And I was thankful that Lance had thought that far ahead with such a sensitive topic. I unbuttoned my suit coat and quickly placed my drink order, then took a seat in front of Lance.

And after placing our food orders, I settled back for the awkward conversation about to happen.

"So, you're interested in having a child," he said.

I sipped my wine. "I have been for some time now."

"How long is *some time*?"

I snickered. "Since I started dating my last ex."

He whistled to himself. "That many years, huh?"

I shrugged. "I thought she was the one, you know? And we had plans to have children, eventually. I was looking forward to being a father, too."

"Until you caught her cheating."

I took a long pull from my glass. "Thanks for the reminder."

He leaned forward, clasping his hands on top of the table. "What if I told you that you wouldn't be the only rich man in this world to consider using a surrogate to become a parent?"

"I'd ask you how many of those men were also single."

"And what if I told you around forty percent of them?"

I almost choked on my wine. "I'm sorry, what?"

He barked with laughter. "Ryan, come on. You think you're the first lonely rich man to consider using a surrogate to have children, even though he doesn't have a woman in his life? Men have biological clocks and needs as well. And it's hard out there for a rich man when it comes to dating. It's hard to weed through the beautiful women who only want your money and the beautiful women who only want the attention the press gives them for being with you. It's much more common than you realize."

I set my glass down. "I'm starting to see that."

While I still felt awkward discussing this topic with such a close friend, it felt good to express this side of me. When I rode, people expected me to be stoic and focused. And when I worked, people expected me to be a tight-wad while I barked out orders. I understood why, though. My family had a reputation for always being streamlined, no matter the cost. So, certain personality stereotypes came with those kinds of reputations.

I just wanted one part of my life to be something *I* wanted.

"Have you always wanted a family?" Lance asked.

The plate with my steak on it touched down in front of me, and I picked up my fork and knife. "Yes, and a big one as well. I mean, I come from a massive family, even if we are blended. And I love it. I wouldn't trade it for anything in the world. They're always there, even if Mom and Dad can't be, and I've always been able to rely on them. I want that for my own children, but I just can't find a woman who's genuine and whose desires line up with my own."

Lance took a bite of his salad. "The women of Dallas will weep when Ryan Remington is officially off the streets because of a newborn in his life."

I rolled my eyes. "Well, they can weep all they want, but if I have a daughter? They'll all be second place, at best."

"Do you want a daughter?"

I smiled at the thought. "A daughter and a son, to start out with. Then, maybe I can build from there."

"This isn't a business, Ryan. It's a family."

I shot him a look. "I'm well aware of that. And since when does my reputation around town affect this sort of thing?"

He shrugged. "You'll want a surrogate who's local, right? Someone you can have easy access to?"

I blinked. "Fuck."

He snickered. "Don't worry about it. I have a doctor friend in this industry—who is fully confidential and above board, by the way—who can hook you up with some down-to-earth women who don't care that you're a handsome, eligible, rich-as-hell, suave older man looking for a new way of life."

I wrinkled my nose. "Is that really my reputation around town?"

"With the men, sure. Most women, however, just talk about the size of your dick."

I almost choked on the piece of steak I was chewing. "I'm sorry, but are you fucking kidding me?"

He threw his head back with laughter. "If people only knew how pious and clueless the almighty Ryan Remington really is."

I shook my head. "Can we try to keep the laughter and the mocking to a minimum? Because I'm serious."

His laughter died down. "I am, too. Kayla and Karlie were born from a surrogate, so I understand exactly where you're sitting."

I almost dropped my fork. "Wait, what?"

He smiled. "My girls, Kayla and Karlie."

"I know who they are, Lance, Jesus. I thought you and Katie had them together?"

He shook his head. "Most people assume that, but no. I met Katie when my surrogate was entering her second trimester. And, like the goddess of a woman she is, she fully accepted that and has been there since they were born."

"And you don't regret it?"

"Not one fucking bit. My girls are my life, and since Katie has a birth defect with her uterus, it's how we've decided to have our third child."

I smiled brightly. "Dude, congratulations. When's the big day?"

"Any day now, actually. Our surrogate was inseminated a week ago, so we have an appointment in a few weeks to see if any of the embryos attached."

"Wow. That's just—wow, Lance. Seriously. I'm really happy for you."

His eyes held mine. "Look, the order in which you have children doesn't matter. Whether or not you have a partner doesn't matter. What matters is your heart. So, where's your heart right now, Ryan? Answer without thinking. Where's your heart?"

I didn't hesitate. "Settling here in Dallas, even though Dallas seems to keep running away from me."

He nodded slowly. "The big city life finally wearing on you?"

I sighed as I leaned back. "I never thought it would, but here we are."

"How about this? Let me set you up with a few different appointments. They can be video conferences if that fits better into your schedule. And that way, you can interview and speak with women who have been through surrogacy before. You can ask them questions and get to know them. And who knows? Maybe you'll find someone you trust and connect with enough to take this journey."

I nodded slowly. "Is that how you started this whole thing? With curious little interviews?"

He winked. "We all have our own paths, Ryan. You don't have to take mine to walk your own. Just know that it's more common than you think, so you need to stop second-guessing yourself. If this is something you want, then take the offer and enjoy the journey."

I drew in a deep breath. "All right, then. Video conferences will work just fine since I'm due back in Conroe in a couple of days. So, just let me know when they're scheduled, and I'll make the time."

He clapped his hands. "Wonderful! Now, let's celebrate with this wonderful food that's growing cold. I'm starving."

We ate, and we drank, and I picked up the tab while we shot the shit. Lance and I didn't get together very often. If anything, we called and texted more than we saw each other. But whenever we finally got together, it was as if things had never been left in the first place.

So, I ended up back at my home office with a smile on my face.

"What's this?" I murmured to myself.

I had an email stating "URGENT" in the subject like from no one other than Bryce himself. I dropped into my leather chair and kicked off my shoes before I clicked on the email. And I only had to scan the first few lines to know what I had to do.

Ryan,

I know this is shitty timing, but something's come up with the refinery. We need all hands on deck to—

I didn't even finish the email. All I did was pull up my schedule, move things around, and notified my virtual secretary that I'd be heading back to Conroe tonight. And after answering a few more emails and confirming times for all sorts of phone calls and shit, I rushed to pack my bags.

Thoughts of the surrogacy and my conversation with Lance that afternoon flew out the window as I hauled my ass downstairs. I locked up my luxury condo and threw my suitcases into the back of my truck that people always teased me for having. Those in Dallas who had money always made sure to flaunt it. They bought the latest Teslas and modified their cars with insane lights and sounds and doors. They turned over their wardrobe every season and had closets stocked with nothing but jewelry and shoes.

But, me? All I needed was my truck, a place to lay my head, and family.

"Let's get this show on the road," I whispered.

I pulled myself up into my truck and set a course for the Rocking R Ranch. I pulled away from my condo complex and started for the highway, readying myself for the next few weeks. There was a lot of work to be done, yes, but also a lot of partying. And it all led up to the one rodeo I'd been working my ass off to attend for the past five years.

It's gonna be a good summer.

And I found myself excited to spend that time with my brothers.

𝒮 6 𝒮

Ellie

I kissed Micah on the head before Miss Weatherford walked him out the door with his diaper bag in tow. I smiled as he pointed to the pool just before the door closed, then I let out a tremendous sigh. Work had been absolute hell this past week, even though I did get paid for a project I had finally finished. But, the two consultations I did certainly didn't go as planned.

And I felt myself falling more than floating.

I dragged myself into the kitchen and threw back a mug of black coffee. The sting and the burn woke me up enough to get a decent shower and throw on some clothes. But, before I could get out the door, I heard someone knocking on it. I rolled my eyes and reached for a bagel, and then I slid my feet into my boots. And without lacing them up, I went to go see who was at my door at a sinful seven-thirty in the morning.

"Yeah?" I asked.

Sadie stood in front of me. "I brought you more coffee from that place you love."

I took a massive bite of my bagel. "I adore you."

She giggled. "Here, take it. They were doing a buy-one-get-one this morning."

I took the coffee from her and washed down the bagel before I stepped outside. She closed the door behind me, and we went to sit on a couple of lounge chairs by the hot tub. I drew in a deep breath while I mindlessly ate my pathetic breakfast with Sadie chomping on some apples and peanut butter next to me.

And as caffeine filled my veins, my thoughts turned to Ryan.

He had simply vanished into thin air after the rodeo last week. He came as quickly as he went nowadays, and I had to admit that part of me was disappointed. I missed out on congratulating him on an event well-run. I missed out on having an excuse to hug him and feel his strong warmth against my body. But, when his laughter caught my ear, my head whipped toward the sound.

Which made Sadie giggle. "Missing Ryan, huh?"

I rolled my eyes. "I just haven't congratulated him yet on the rodeo. He left before I caught him the next morning."

"Leave it to him, I suppose. He's practically a ghost some-times, isn't he?"

I caught Ryan's figure around the left side of the house, and I furrowed my brow. He was all smiles and laughter as he reached out his arms, and that's when I saw someone giving him a hug. I leaned over a bit into Sadie's lap to try to figure out who the hell had that man so cheerfully happy at this ungodly hour of the morning.

But, I didn't recognize the person he was embracing. "Who is that?" I asked.

Sadie gasped. "Oh! You haven't met his brothers yet!"

I quirked an eyebrow. "Wait, what?"

She pushed me off her. "That's Wyatt. Boone's probably already in the kitchen, eating something, but yeah. Those are his brothers."

"I thought Bryce and Will and Bart were his brothers."

"Those are his half-brothers. From Remington senior's previous marriage."

I blinked. "I didn't know there was a previous marriage."

She nodded. "Oh, yeah! He was married once and had Ryan, Wyatt, and Boone; then they divorced amicably, and he remarried who you know as Mrs. Remington now, and them two had Bryce, Will, and Bart."

"Huh."

She smiled. "Guess the whole family's in town for the summer now."

My eyes trailed back to Ryan, and I watched him embrace another man who had what looked like a sandwich in his hand. That must've been Boone, and I noticed how much younger everyone looked compared to Ryan. I mean, that didn't bother me one bit. I thought he wore the salted hair at his temples and the gray of his tailored beard very, very well.

Sadie nudged me. "Staring at old Uncle Ryan again, I see."

I took a long pull from my coffee. "The man isn't old, Sadie. He's only forty or so."

I heard someone rushing toward us in the grass, and I turned to see Luna running as quickly as she could. She held her cell phone in the air and squealed before she dropped down onto the concrete between the two lounge chairs, completely oblivious to the fact that it was now only eight in the morning.

"Guys! Guys, guys, guys. Guess. What?" she asked.

I blinked. "You brought more food?"

Sadie barked with laughter as I shoved the last of my bagel into my mouth.

"No, silly," Luna said, "Bella's coming into town."

I blinked. "Who?"

Sadie gasped. "Wait, since when?"

Luna giggled profusely. "Since now! She just called me to tell me. She's coming for the whole summer, at least!"

"Oh my God!"

Sadie shot up from her chair and embraced Luna while I sat there, looking like a confused frog on a lilypad. "Sorry, does someone want to fill me in?"

Willow walked up behind us, giggling. "She's Luna's child-hood best friend, way back in elementary school. And she's coming to replace us because Luna doesn't love us anymore."

I chuckled as Luna's face fell. "Hey, she's not replacing

anyone. And don't worry, you guys are gonna *love* her. She's just like us."

Sadie grinned. "So, she enjoys late-night snacks and movies?"

Willow smiled brightly. "And cotton candy in all sorts of flavors."

I cleared my throat. "And slamming a hammer against molten metal to mold it into the shape of a penis?"

The girls all stared at me as if I'd grown a third arm.

"So, that's a no?" I asked.

Luna giggled. "You're so silly. I love that about you, Ellie."

Sadie swatted my shoulder. "You can poke fun all you want, but I'm excited to get a little more estrogen in this sausage fest that the ranch has become."

"Amen!" Willow exclaimed.

I snorted at her remark. "You've got that right."

Sadie sighed. "I mean, even the majority of the horses are male! Come on now."

Luna clapped her hands. "And the best part? I've already invited her to the barn party, and she is a beautician so she can do our hair and our makeup and our nails!"

The girls squealed and jumped with delight as I sat there, finishing off the last of my coffee. I had no idea how the fuck they had this much energy so early in the morning, but I needed to find a way to bottle it.

Maybe I could sell that shit and make a ton of money instead of sweating my ass off with hot equipment all damn day.

"Doesn't that sound exciting, Ellie?" Sadie asked.

I felt all of them looking at me as I nodded. "Yeah, that sounds great."

Luna jumped with joy. "All right, I'm going to go call Bella back and let her know she's got eager clients. Bye, guys!"

Willow dropped into the lounge chair on my other side. "I need another cup of coffee just to replenish after all that."

Sadie fell back into her chair. "You got that right."

I thumbed behind me. "Want me to go make another pot? Micah's molars have finally come in, so I don't feel like a complete zombie this morning."

Sadie scoffed. "You think teething's hard? Try doing teeth with twins."

Willow held up her hand. "You can take the cake with that one. I wouldn't wish that kind of hell on my worst enemy."

I finished off the coffee Sadie had brought me. "The thing that made it the worst was that the Orajel numbing stuff you suggested? It didn't work."

Willow slowly looked over at me. "What?"

I nodded. "Didn't fucking work. And there were some all-nighters in there, too."

Sadie raised herself up. "Nope. You need someone to make the pot after that admission. I can't even imagine what I'd do if that stuff didn't work on the twins."

I giggled as Sadie patted my shoulder, then she headed into the guesthouse. I checked my watch on my wrist and saw it was only eight-thirty, and I breathed a sigh of relief. On Fridays, I didn't report to my office until ten, and I was out of there by three. I intentionally made those my shorter days because I almost always had to work on Saturdays. So, I wanted some semblance of a weekend.

I found my gaze gravitating back over to where Ryan had once been. I searched for him in the shadows of the house before my stomach dropped. He wasn't there anymore, and disappointment wafted around in my gut.

But, I didn't bury it quickly enough before Willow called me out. "Excited that he's back?"

I groaned. "I hate all of you sometimes."

She snickered. "You make it easy for us. You practically drool when the guy is around."

I clicked my tongue. "I do not."

"You really, really do. I wouldn't be shocked if he's seen it himself."

I looked over at him. "Wait, you think he's seen me?"

Sadie came back out while Willow laughed. "Coffee's up!"

She divvied out the warm mugs, and I drew in a deep breath of its miraculous scent. "What's so funny?" she asked as she sat back in her lounger.

Willow sipped her cream-colored drink. "Just teasing Ellie about her crush."

Sadie propped her mug against her thigh. "Did Ryan come back out or something?"

I rolled my eyes. "Okay, you guys can stop now."

"But why?" Willow asked in a fake-whiny voice. "It's so much fun, Ellie!"

I groaned. "Now, I really hate you."

Sadie clutched her heart in feigned pain. "Whatever will we do without you?"

I couldn't help but smile as my eyes fell to the back of the house. I saw Ryan walking around in the kitchen, talking and laughing with his two other brothers. I hadn't met them yet, and I wondered for a split second if it would be weird to walk inside and introduce myself.

"I would at least take a shower before you do," Willow said.

My head whipped toward her. "What?"

She grinned. "I'm not stupid, nor am I new to this game. You're thinking about going inside and using the brothers you don't know as an excuse to be around Ryan."

Sadie piped up on the other side of me. "I mean, it's creative, I'll give you that."

My face fell. "I'm going back inside."

Willow gripped my arm. "Come on, quit being so hard on us. I, personally, think it's cute."

Sadie giggled. "It really is. I've never seen you so smitten before. I mean, except with—"

I peered over my shoulder and shot her a dangerous look. "Don't you dare bring him up."

Willow blinked. "Uh, oh. An ex?"

Sadie whispered loudly, "Micah's father."

I ripped away from Willow. "Seriously. Shut the fuck up about him."

Sadie murmured. "Okay, okay, fine. Damn."

Willow scoffed, "Maybe you should think about resolving

those feelings before you hop onto feelings for someone else, though."

I had half a mind to throw my hot ass coffee in her face, but she had a point. So, all I did was march my happy ass back inside. I closed the door behind me and locked it for good measure, then pressed my back against the wall.

Sometimes, putting on a brave face was hard.

I tried not to be a bitch sometimes, but it was difficult. These girls were nothing like me, and their lives were nothing like mine. Willow and Sadie got to live out their days with the men they loved. With the men who had given them their children. But, not all of us were so lucky. Being a single mother was, hands down, the hardest thing about my life, and sometimes I wondered if I needed to go get a regular job and suck up the fact that my passion might not be worth it.

I closed my eyes and drew in a few deep breaths to calm my racing heart.

Ever since I had moved in, Miss Weatherford had offered her services to me, free of charge. And when I had found out Will was compensating her behind my back, it had infuriated me. This family was giving me so much help and so much love, and I couldn't even get my damn business up and running. I couldn't even pay them back for the generosity they kept bestowing upon me, and it made me irate. Miss Weatherford kept Micah while I worked; the Remington Brothers had purchased all of the heavy equipment and gear I needed while also providing me an office. Bryce was letting me stay in the guesthouse free of charge in exchange for my farrier services. It all felt like too much sometimes.

"I have to find a way to make this work," I whispered to myself.

Will's justification for helping me out was that he didn't want any woman's dreams to be put on the back burner just because of children. Like Sadie and her petting zoo, or Willow and her own racing schedule. Will always told me he was "only being fair" when it came to covering the nannying costs so I could set regular hours in my shop.

But as the months ticked by, I felt myself forever failing on my end of the bargain.

"A cold shower. That'll snap me out of this," I hissed.

If there was one thing I had learned during my years of training in Dallas, it was this—people always came back for the best. So, what I had to do in Conroe was position myself as the best. Even though I couldn't sell my products at retail prices, and even though I couldn't churn things out as quickly as manufacturing plants, that didn't mean I still couldn't build a reputation as the best in town.

The first step in that plan, however, was finding recurring clients.

Which was quickly proving to be the most challenging part of this game.

I charged into the bathroom and turned on the cold water before ripping off my pajamas. I stepped into the cold stream, allowing it to shock me from my negative frame of mind. I couldn't go to work distracted because that was when real injuries happened. That was when people died on the job, and the thought of Micah losing me made my eyes water.

I shivered as I ran the cold water through my hair before quickly switching it to warm. And the second I did, I heard his laughter reverberating through the walls.

Ryan was talking with the girls outside.

I found myself focusing on the rumbling tones of his laughter rather than the shampoo I needed to put into my hair.

7

Ryan

"So, when are you going to start training with Monty before the championship rodeo?" Wyatt asked.

I shook my head. "There goes my brother, already buckling down and being serious."

Boone threw his arm over Wyatt's shoulder. "Come on, man, loosen up a little. Old Man Ryan here just beat out every single youngster in his category! Let the man enjoy it a little."

Wyatt shrugged off his arm. "That's fine for you, but I'm always focused on the future. We have a lot to brush up on, and even more to get in order before the rodeo even comes around! And I'm not just talking about training."

I rolled my eyes. "Work talk on the weekend? How very Wyatt of you."

He glared at me. "You can poke fun all you want, but my being serious is what keeps all of us in line sometimes."

Boone snickered. "Think whatever you want, but we all know the reason why you're much too serious."

Wyatt glared at him. "And why's that, asshole?"

I stepped in the middle of them. "Whoa-ho-ho-ho! No name-calling necessary for now. Wyatt, you know we're just having a bit of fun."

Boone patted my shoulder. "You also know that we'll buckle down once the time comes around, so get your panties out of your ass."

Wyatt reached for his neck, but I blocked his efforts. I picked Wyatt up clear over my shoulder and spun him around, causing everyone outside to start laughing. The girls included. And while I knew it was fun to rile up Wyatt and watch him tear people to shreds with nothing but his words, I didn't want any of that happening today. We all needed to be happy with the prosperity we had as a family.

"Put me down!" Wyatt exclaimed.

I set him back onto his feet and smacked his ass. "Come on. I'll get you a beer."

He scoffed. "You know I don't drink beer when I'm on the clock."

Boone looked at his watch. "Since when are you on the clock at three in the afternoon on a Saturday?"

Wyatt's face fell. "It's Friday, idiot. And it's definitely nine in the morning."

I chuckled. "Beers for everyone! We're calling in sick today, Wyatt."

He sighed. "I shouldn't be surprised one bit."

Boone smirked. "Put some whiskey in his beer! Man needs to lighten up a little bit."

The girls fell apart in laughter in their lounge chairs, but a part of me wished that Ellie were out there with them. I enjoyed her presence and her laughter. She had this cute way of wrinkling her nose whenever she couldn't stop giggling, and the wheezing sound she made if someone really got her going always made me laugh even harder.

She was contagious, that woman. And I wanted to be around her more now that I was back in Conroe.

"You see this?" Wyatt asked. He thrust his cell phone in my face before pulling it away.

"Uh, see what? You didn't even give my eyes time to focus," I said.

He frowned deeply. "It's Mr. Higglebaum, from our board of investors? Remember them? This would be the reason why I don't morning-drink like my lush brothers because one of us has to pick up these phone calls."

Boone nodded. "Well, go on. Pick it up."

Wyatt's glare that he shot Boone could have killed the man. "Eat shit, Boone."

My brother smiled. "Get laid, Wyatt."

I turned Wyatt to face me. "Go take the call inside. I'll be in there in a second to help."

He nodded. "At least someone wants to contribute around here."

I breathed a sigh of relief as Wyatt walked away and took the call. But, I knew I needed to be right behind him. Wyatt had a nasty mouth on him whenever he got angry, and the last thing I needed was him bitching out the wrong person on our board. I shot Boone a warning look before I followed Wyatt into the kitchen, quickly lunging for the phone before he said something too harshly.

And while Wyatt fought for his phone back, I cleared my throat.

"Mr. Higglebaum! It's so good to hear from you this morning," I said.

He paused. "Ryan? What happened to Wyatt?"

Wyatt hissed, "Give me that back."

I placed my hand against his face and pushed him back. "He had to go to the bathroom. Morning coffee and all. I'm sure you understand."

Wyatt growled, "I'm going to kill you."

Mr. Higglebaum chuckled. "Trust me, I know the feeling. I wanted to go ahead and call to get an update on things since I heard you were back in town. For good, I hope?"

I knew our investors were gunning to get me back in Conroe, but it wasn't that simple. Moving back home took time, organization, and—most of all—finding the right space. I didn't want just any old place here in Conroe. Most of the houses were dilapidated and falling apart, and if I were going to sink that kind of money into a home, I might as well build something new.

Except there wasn't much ground to break in this small town that wasn't already owned by a rancher utilizing it.

Boone whispered, "Wyatt, get the hell off him, man."

I heard my brothers tussling behind me as I focused on the phone call. "I'm working as quickly as I can to rectify that, but realty does take some time."

Mr. Higglebaum barked with laughter. "Don't I know it. Took my wife and me almost two years to close on the house we're in now. Can you believe that? Two years!"

Jesus, I hope it doesn't take that long. "It's a beautiful home, though. I'm sure it was worth it."

"Worth every penny and then some!"

I sat down at the kitchen table as Boone dragged Wyatt outside. "So, what can I do for you this morning?"

"Well, I was calling Wyatt specifically to talk about the returns we can expect for this quarter. He said we'd have graphs and all that shit in our inboxes by Monday, but I was hoping for a yay or nay on that ten percent growth he promised us last quarter.

I turned and gazed at the porch door as Wyatt scrambled to get back inside. "I'd love to report on that, but we try not to favor anyone on our investor's board over anyone else. The order in which we asked for donations going toward the refinery was simply due to the alphabetical listing of numbers in our phone book, so to speak. But, once Wyatt is done spending time with family and throwing back a few beers, I'm sure he wouldn't mind giving you a call Sunday evening?"

Wyatt yelled from the doorway, "I'm going to kill you!"

Mr. Higglebaum paused. "Who was that?"

I turned my back to the door. "Boone and Wyatt rough-housing. It's been a while since we've all been together."

"Well, don't let me keep you from family, then! And let Wyatt know I'll be anxiously awaiting a call Sunday evening."

I stood to my feet. "Good speaking with you! And tell Rosemary I said hello."

"Will do, Ryan. Take care and enjoy time with the family!"

"And you as well!"

Wyatt yanked the phone from my hand and held it up to his ear. "Give me that. Mr. Higglebaum? Mr. Higglebaum!"

I smiled triumphantly. "He's eagerly awaiting a phone call from you Sunday evening. And you know what happens when you call a man like that before his requested appointment."

I honestly thought tightwad Wyatt's head was going to blow through the damn roof. But instead, he stormed out of the kitchen, grumbling to himself.

"You think we should go easy on him?" Boone asked as he walked up to my side. "I mean, the man just loves his business."

I shrugged. "Once he shotguns a beer, I'll be good."

Wyatt threw the remote control down the hallway. "I can hear you both, you imbeciles!"

Boone and I ducked as we started laughing our asses off. Man, when Wyatt really got going, it was practically a spin-out session. And I'd never find anything funnier than Wyatt getting so worked up over a simple phone call.

Boone lowered his voice. "We better get back outside before he skins us alive."

Wyatt yelled back at us, "And roasts you fuckers on a spit!"

I chuckled as I stood, then offered my hand to Boone. "Come on, let's head outside. Maybe the girls are still out there."

We made our way back through the kitchen and grabbed a few beers in the process. But, when we stepped out onto the porch, Boone and I found ourselves alone. Well, not necessarily alone, but Sadie was walking off in the direction of her place while Luna strutted for the porch.

"Want a beer?" Boone asked as she passed.

Luna giggled. "No, thanks. It's a wine kind of morning for me."

I cracked open a beer for myself. "Seems to be that kind of day for everyone."

Boone dropped himself into a porch chair. "Why do you think Wyatt is the way he is?"

I pulled up a chair beside him. "Ah, you know him, he's always taken after Mom."

"In every bad way, sure."

I sipped my drink. "I mean, the good ways, too. If you're ever sick or down for the count, Wyatt's the one you want taking care of you, that's for sure."

"I just wish he'd lighten up a bit. He can really be a mood-killer."

I clinked my beer bottle against his. "Hear fucking hear to that."

Luna pulled up a seat across the porch table from us and poured some red wine into a red solo cup, and the picture made me grin.

"You doing okay over there?" I asked.

She looked over at me. "What? Do we really have to keep it classy when it's just family?"

Boone held up his beer bottle. "I knew I liked you. To new beginnings!"

Luna held up her cup. "To a loving family and good food!"

I held up my own drink. "And to memories that last a lifetime."

Just as we cheered our drinks, the guesthouse door opened. And when Ellie emerged, my focus was solely on her. I watched her blond hair billow behind her before she pulled it into a low ponytail. Her jeans clung to her luscious curves that called to my fingertips, and her hips swayed so beautifully that my mouth started filling with spit. I craved her some days: the scent of her body wash, or the soft touch of her hand whenever she laid it against my forearm to catch my attention. There wasn't a damn thing about that woman that didn't strike me as absolute perfection.

But, every time I made a move toward her, I watched a wall go up over her face.

Who hurt you, Ellie?

"Stare much?" Luna asked with a giggle.

I tossed back the rest of my beer. "Can't help it if she's right in front of me."

Boone snickered. "Yeah, yeah. Whatever you say, my man."

Luna grinned. "She's got a few secrets of her own, you know. Secrets you might want to know someday."

My ears perked up. "Care to indulge a couple of them, Luna?"

She grabbed her bottle of wine and stood. "Not in the slightest. You boys have a good day, now! And I'll see you guys at dinner tonight."

Boone nudged me. "You think she means that Ellie's got a crush on your or something?"

I shrugged as I watched her leave. "I don't know, but I do know one thing."

"You're going to find out?"

I looked over at my brother with a smirk. "I'm going to find *all* of them out."

8

Ellie

Willow kept throwing T-shirts out of my closet. "No. No. No. Oh, hell, no. And no."

Luna wrinkled her nose. "Why do you have your T-shirts hanging up in the closet?"

I blinked. "Because I don't want them to get wrinkled."

Willow sighed. "Your closet is for nice things, not loungewear."

I blinked again. "My T-shirts *are* my nice things."

Willow spun around. "You're kidding."

I shook my head. "No."

Sadie groaned. "See why I asked you guys to come over to help? She's got no idea how to get ready for something like this."

I looked over at her. "Something like a barn dance? Don't I just put on some jeans, my boots, a hat, and then go dance?"

Luna giggled. "The guys do, sure. But, not the girls."

Willow turned back to my closet. "Do you even have a skirt in here? Because all I see are ripped jeans."

I shrugged. "What's wrong with ripped jeans?"

Sadie sighed. "Oh my goodness. This is going to be rough."

Luna stood and held out her hand. "Come on. While they pick out your outfit, I can get started on your hair and makeup."

I shot my gaze up to hers. "No."

She cocked her head. "No, to what?"

"To both of them. No makeup and my hair is fine like it is."

Willow scoffed, "You aren't going to the first barn dance of the summer with a knotted bun on top of your head. Now, get in Luna's chair and shut up so she can work."

My eyebrows rose, and I almost fired back, except Sadie placed her hand in mine. She squeezed it, and I looked over at her. There was something behind her eyes that gave me pause.

"Why is this so important to you guys?" I asked.

Sadie scooted closer to me. "Will you trust me? Just this once?"

Willow shrieked, "Yes!"

I jumped at the sound before she tossed a gray, floral-print dress that I thought I had thrown away onto the bed.

"No," I said.

Willow spun around. "You're wearing it with your freshly shined boots, and that's an order."

I slowly stood to my feet. "This dress belongs in the trash. I thought I'd already gotten rid of it. I'm not wearing it tonight."

Sadie stood to her feet. "Please? Just for the night?"

I looked over at her and lowered my voice. "You know why I don't like this dress."

She gave me her best puppy dog eyes. "I'll make the fire you can throw it into before we roast marshmallows after the dance tonight. Okay? I'll pack you another pair of clothes, you can come over to my place, and we'll have a bonfire with s'mores while we burn your dress."

Willow interjected. "Uh, sorry, but why don't we like the dress?"

My face fell. "My ex gave it to me."

Luna bounded up beside me, taking my hand. "Well, it's only for one night. And if you wear it, I promise I'll keep your makeup and hair to a minimum."

I quirked an eyebrow. "And no jewelry?"

"I'll compromise with dangling earrings and no necklace. How's that sound?"

I turned to face her. "No crazy makeup colors?"

Luna held up her hand. "Scout's honor."

I paused. "Were you ever a scout?"

She sighed. "I promise on my life, girl. Okay?"

I licked my lips. "Okay, fine. I'll wear the dress."

The girls burst into giggling and clapping as Luna tugged

me over to the seat she had in front of a mirror. It was hair first, and I had to admit that her brushing it felt terrific. I knew I wouldn't feel like myself all night, but I also wanted to be part of this little dynamic they had going on. And if it were that important to them for me to dress up, then I would.

But I didn't have to like it.

See, the barn dance was out in an old abandoned barn building that Bryce, Will, and Bart had revamped on their own time. Now, the barn wasn't used as a stable or storage facility at all. They used it strictly to host dinner parties and dances and birthday engagements so they wouldn't have to keep renting out spaces in town. It was pretty ingenious, considering the fact that this family *loved* their parties. But, it was out among the woods of their property with nothing but a cobblestone walkway to usher someone up to the front of the barn. And I'd be walking all that way—in a dress and sweating my makeup off in this humid nighttime heat.

Nevertheless, I had to admit that I looked pretty good. My shiny brown boots had faded brass accents with cream-colored stitching against the leather. It went well with the gray floral dress I had on, and pale-yellow dangling earrings Luna had hung from my ears brought a pop of color without the harshness.

And damn it, it almost looked like I wasn't wearing makeup at all except for my crimson-red lips.

"So, what do you think?" Sadie asked.

I gazed at myself in the mirror. "I think it's going to feel nice to burn this dress for good."

Willow clapped. "I'll take it! Now, come on. The rest of us have thirty minutes to piece ourselves together before we head out."

I figured they would at least walk there with me, but once they finished getting ready in the guesthouse, their men started picking them up. Bryce came to get Willow first, then Bart came for Luna. And finally, Will came with Mrs. Weatherford so she could look after the children at my place while we were all at the party.

"You want to walk with us?" Sadie asked.

I shook my head. "You guys go on ahead. I'm going to get Mrs. Weatherford settled, then I'll be down there."

"You sure?" Will asked.

I shooed them out the door. "Go on and stop worrying about me. I'm good, I promise."

There was the smallest part of me that thought about backing out. I mean, there wasn't anyone in my guesthouse to stop me. But, Micah always had a wonderful time playing with the twins, and I didn't want to rob him of a fun-filled evening.

So, I left and started making the trek for the cobblestone path.

There were warm-white lights strung up on either side of the pathway, softly illuminating the forestry around me. The lights and the cobblestone pathway led me right to the front of the massive barn double doors that were open and filled with music, food, and people. The amazing smells alone made my mouth water as I approached. The clopping of boots against hardwood called to me, making me feel right at home while people slung back drinks and bellied up to the bar for their whiskey neats and glasses of sangria. People everywhere whooped and hollered, and it tugged a soft smile across my cheeks as I stepped through the threshold.

And when the crowd parted, ushering me inside, there stood Ryan.

On the dance floor.

In the tightest pair of jeans I'd ever seen on a man.

I watched as he swiveled his hips and stomped his boots on the rugged hardwood floor. Hay trickled from the rafters, falling through the slats like a Southern country snowfall. Ryan's rolled-up button-front shirt sat in the crook of his bicep, accenting just how strong his arms were.

And when his eyes met mine, they stole my breath away.

I felt rooted to my place as Ryan stopped dancing. I watched him as he brushed off other women and made his way off the dance floor. He plucked a couple of drinks off a passing tray, and I could have sworn he was making his way for me.

Don't fuck it up. Don't fuck it up. Don't fuck it—

"You look incredible tonight, Ellie," he said. He handed me the glass of red wine, and I took it.

"You don't look half bad yourself, cowboy."

He grinned. "I try when I can."

You don't even have to try. "Congratulations on your win, by the way. I never got a chance to say that to you."

"And I never got a chance to thank you for your quick

work on Monty. Had you not been there, I wouldn't have taken that top spot."

I sipped my drink. "Just doing my job. You don't need to thank me for that."

He took a step toward me. "Then, thank you for rushing the field and showing that you care. That, alone, means just as much."

I felt my cheeks heating. "Again, just my job. I'm really glad you're okay, though."

He smirked as he leaned back. "You hungry?"

I released the breath I didn't know I had been holding. "Actually, I could use a bite to eat."

He offered me his arm. "Come with me. I think the line to the buffet has finally died down."

The second I threaded my arm through his, I felt my heart stop in my chest. I threw back the rest of my wine, chugged it down, and then set the drink on an empty table. We went through the buffet line and got a bite to eat before he retrieved us a couple more drinks. The banter back and forth between us felt almost natural.

Then, he asked me for the unnatural. "Care to dance, Ellie?"

I almost choked on the last of my second glass of wine. "I'm sorry, what?"

He chuckled. "Dance. You know, that thing you do down on the floor? Care to dance for a few songs?"

I blinked. "I, uh..."

He smirked. "Don't tell me you don't dance, Elliebear."

My voice caught in my throat. "Elliebear?"

He stood and offered me his hand. "Come on. I'll teach you."

I stared at his hand as if he had grown a second thumb.

"Well? Don't keep me waiting, beautiful. Come on!"

The second I placed his hand into mine, he ripped me up from the chair. He scooped me into his arms with effortless ease as the alcohol settled into my veins. I felt as light as a feather without a care in the world. And when he placed me onto my feet in the middle of the dance floor, a slow song came on.

"Oh, this'll be easy. Put your arms around my neck," Ryan said.

I rolled my eyes. "I know how to slow dance."

He slithered his arms around the small of my back. "Then, let's get to it."

Off and on, we danced, interchanging slow songs with country jigs that he knew every single dance to. He taught me some, and I caught on pretty quickly, but there were others where all I did was step on his toes. Nevertheless, he was a fantastic sport, and by the end of the evening, we were five drinks deep and stumbling outside to get some fresh air.

"Oh, that feels so good," I groaned.

Ryan leaned against the outside of the building. "I love cool Texas nights."

The wind kicked up, and I drew in a deep breath. "Ain't enough of 'em sometimes, ya know?"

He chuckled. "Sounds like someone's accent gets stronger the more they drink."

I held my finger up. "*Ssshhh!* It's our little secret."

"Come here, you." He reached for my waist and pulled me toward him, away from the lights and the crowd and the chaos. With his back leaning against the barn with that cool swagger of his, his hands settled against my hips as his legs spread.

Accommodating my stance as I placed my head against the swell of his chest.

"This feels nice," he murmured.

I felt him kiss the top of my head, and my heart soared with delight. "It's very nice, yes."

His hands started bunching up my dress. "Might lead to other nice things, if both parties consent."

A shiver shot down my spine as I looked up into his eyes. "I can't, I'm sorry."

His hands immediately dropped. "No, my apologies. I'm definitely—"

I pressed my finger against his lips. "Stop talking and listen. I have the nanny at the guesthouse for the night with the kids. I just meant I've got nowhere for us to go. That's all."

He kissed the tip of my finger. "You're a city-country girl, aren't ya?"

I blinked. "What?"

He wrapped his hand around my wrist. "Lemme guess—

born and raised in one of the big three. That's to say Houston, San Antonio, or Dallas. Right?"

I drew in a curt breath. "I mean, on the outskirts of Dallas. But, still."

He took my hand. "Come with me then."

I spun around as he moved me. "Where are we going?"

"Just come on and quit askin' questions."

He tugged me off the cobblestone path and into the woods, and we didn't stop walking until the lights of the pathway were nothing but a soft glow on the horizon. Critters skittered beneath our feet, and the soft breeze rustled the green leaves above our heads. And before I knew it, Ryan had my body pinned to the trunk of a massive tree with his knee between my legs.

"Now, what was that you were sayin' about some guesthouse?" he asked.

The low notes of his voice rattled my stomach and made my heart seize in my chest. "I–I, uh..."

He chuckled. "That's what I thought, beautiful."

And before I could get another word in edgewise, his lips crushed my own.

My tongue found his, and I crashed into his web of utter and luxurious debauchery.

9

Ryan

The second her tongue invaded my mouth, all bets were off. I gripped her hips and hoisted her against the tree with the soft pulsing of the music in the background. My cock stiffened against my jeans. Her hands knocked my hat off and threaded quickly through my hair. I dragged my lips down her neck, kissing and licking and sucking. Marking her pulse point and feeling her roll against me with a wanton lust that matched the fire coursing through my veins.

Finally, I'd have the woman I'd been dreaming about for months.

My hands ran up and down her clothed body, and I silently cursed myself for drinking so much. I knew this wouldn't take long, and I hoped to prove myself enough to her to earn a repeat performance. I tugged at her dress with my teeth, exposing her breasts so I could pull them out. And as I lapped at her puckered peaks, I felt her wet panties rubbing against my cock.

"Oh, shit. Ryan, please."

Her sounds made me growl. It sent shot a thunder through my veins and stuffed my stomach full with a need I'd never felt in my entire life. I shoved up her dress and pinned her to the tree with my torso long enough to pull out my cock. And as my jeans sank to my knees, freeing my leaking thickness for the darkness to behold, I slid her panties off to the side before running my cock up and down her wet little slit.

"You want this?" I asked.

She sucked on my lower lip. "You better make a move before I do, big boy."

I chuckled as I inched myself inside of her, feeling her tremble at my intrusion. Goddammit, this woman was tighter than a freshly dried T-shirt, and I already felt my balls twitching. Her juices slid down my length, venturing toward my balls in an effortless race to see which droplet got there first. And as I buried my face into the crook of her neck, I felt her legs lock even tighter around me, sliding the last inch or so deep inside of her.

"Holy shit," she whispered.

I kissed her skin. "You feel so amazing." I drew my hips

back and slammed into her, feeling her tits bounce against me.

Ellie's head fell back against the tree as I started my rhythmic assault, trying to cover up the fact that the world was tilting around me. Dammit, why the hell had I had so much to drink? I had to learn to control myself around this kind of shit.

Especially if I had my eye on a pretty little thing such as Ellie.

"So close. So close. Ryan, please. Don't stop. Don't fucking stop."

I fisted her hair and pulled it off to the side, exposing her neck. And when I laid my teeth against her, I felt her crumble around me. Her pussy milked my dick, her body quaking as I felt my balls pull into my body. I tried with all my might to fight it. I tried to think about dead skunks and rotten eggs and anything else to get my body to stop the inevitable.

But, the second her pussy held me within its grasp, I was a goner. "Oh, shit," I growled.

I rutted against her, feeling the drunken beast inside me rattle against the bars of its cage. I felt her juices dripping down my balls, coating the skin of my thighs in her marks. She fell limp against the tree as I licked against her skin, kissing the indentations my teeth left behind and hoping she didn't hate me for the mark I knew it would leave.

"Holy hell," she said breathlessly.

I smirked against her exposed collarbone. "Took the words right outta my mouth."

Reluctantly, I slid from between her legs. I set her down onto her feet and held her hips tightly, making sure she had her legs beneath her first. Even with my cock dangling help-lessly between my legs, I felt more powerful and more alive than ever before. And with the alcohol that still rushed through my veins, all inhibitions had been tossed out the window.

"Dammit, you're beautiful," I whispered.

Her eyes met mine before she blushed. "Thank you, that's very nice of you to say."

I tucked a strand of hair behind her ear. "I mean it, you know."

She giggled. "I, uh... I should probably go home and clean myself up. I don't think I'm fit to go back into the party."

I grinned. "Or you could come with me back to my place, and we could take a shower together."

I waited for the cute little "yes" to pour from her lips, but instead, I watched that wall come slamming down over her face. I furrowed my brow as she slithered out from between me and the tree, backtracking as I pulled my pants up my legs.

I walked after her while I fastened my belt and started looking around for my hat. But, the more I moved, the quicker she moved.

"Wait a sec—Ellie! Have you seen my hat?"

She thumbed over her shoulder. "Over there, next to the big rock on the ground."

I scooped it up and rushed after her, gripping her arm. "Wait a second. Would you just stop?"

She whipped around to face me. "I told you that I have to get home."

"And I ain't stoppin' you from doing that. I'm just offering for you to come back to my place and have a bit more fun before you do. That's all."

She shook her head. "Mrs. Weatherford isn't an overnight babysitter, and I'm sure it's closer to one in the morning than we think it is. I just have to get home to relieve her."

That's good, right? "Then, at least let me walk you home."

"I don't know if my son is up or something like that—"

My hand slid down her arm until our fingers found each other. "I've been wanting to formally meet your son for a while now, anyway."

She blinked. "You have?"

I shrugged. "I mean, I've seen him in passing. Cooed at him whenever he's playing with Will's kids. But, I haven't formally met him yet, no."

Something akin to shock passed behind her eyes, and I went to push the conversation further, but her hand pulled away from mine. She turned her back to me and started jogging for the cobblestone pathway, but something in my gut told me not to follow her.

"I had a good time!" I exclaimed.

She held a thumb up in the air. "Me too, Ryan. A great time."

"Maybe next time I can bring coffee and breakfast for you and the little man!"

"Not a good time right now, Ryan!"

I sighed as I watched her form fade into the darkness. I sucked air through my teeth and looked around, wondering if anyone had witnessed my complete and epic failure to seal any kind of deal that promised me more time with her in the future. I scratched my head before sliding my hat back on and turned to face the barn, but the smell of her glorious pussy wafted up to my nose, making me want even more of her.

Go home and take a shower. You need one.

I didn't want to wash away her scent, though. I didn't want to wash away the feeling of her hands, or her lips, or her kiss, or her cries of ecstasy. I wanted to hang onto the memory as long as I could before it grew distant with every passing day. But, I knew I couldn't go back to the barn dance smelling like this.

So, I made the long, sad trek back to my loft over the training stables.

Longing and hoping that I'd get another chance to prove myself to Ellie.

🦋 10 🦋

Ellie

I didn't stop walking, and I didn't pick my head up until I stood on the guesthouse's porch. And every time I reached for the doorknob, I paused. I drew in deep breaths to try to calm the trembling in my hands. I closed my eyes and forced my legs to grow stronger, despite the fact that they felt like jelly.

"Did that just really happen?" I whispered to myself.

I slowly opened my eyes and felt the squishiness of my panties. It made me grimace, but the soft throbbing of my neck caused my hand to fly to my skin. I felt the indents of Ryan's teeth as they marked me. I felt his arousal dripping against my cloth panties and dampening the skin of my thighs.

Had I really just hooked up with the hottest guy at that dance? Against a tree? In the woods?

I turned to face the pool and stared at the muted reflection of the crescent moon. I slowly walked to the water's edge and peered over it, staring down into my own face. The shock on my features took me by surprise. The flush of my cheeks that was still apparent made the rest of my body glow with embarrassment. I hadn't been with a man since I told my ex I had gotten pregnant. I hadn't even entertained the idea of being with a man until Ryan came along.

Did he really mean that comment about Micah?

I let my fingers dance across my swollen lips, chapped and chaffed from kissing him so hard. A soft smile crept across my face as that question of his repeated in my head. Over and over, like the most romantic song that had been composed solely for my ears.

He wanted to meet Micah.

He wanted to meet my boy, personally.

He could be saying that just to get some more of you.

I swallowed hard and turned away from the pool. I started for the front door and let myself in, peeking around the corner to see what was going on. The microwave clock ticked over to 12:43 just as I stepped into the guesthouse. And when I closed the door behind me, a voice rose from the darkness.

"You're back earlier than I thought," Mrs. Weatherford said.

I almost jumped out of my skin as the door slammed behind me.

"Sh-sh-sh-sh! I just got him back to sleep. Poor thing's having nightmares tonight."

I walked over to where she was on the couch. "How many times did he get up this time?"

She shrugged. "Just once, which is good for him, or so I hear. Poor thing was trembling and murmuring about monsters in his closet."

"Did you try the monster spray I keep in his bedside table?"

She nodded. "I also tried turning on the closet light and keeping the door cracked for him. He still woke up."

I sighed, patting her knee. "Thank you for doing your best and thank you for watching him. But where are the twins?"

She grinned. "Sadie and Will picked them up about thirty minutes ago."

My heart stopped in my chest. They'd already left the party? Which way did they go? Where did they walk to?

Did they hear Ryan and me?

Mrs. Weatherford stood to her feet. "Don't feel bad, I was honestly prepared to stay the night. So, keep that in your back pocket the next time you'd like to go out."

I stood and walked her to the front door. "I will and thank you again. I'll ever be able to thank you enough for what you're doing for my son and me."

She patted my shoulder. "Life is hard for all of us. It's why we always have to have each other's backs."

I nodded. "Truer words have never been spoken."

She eyed me carefully. "Anything you want to talk about?"

Get her out. Now. "No, why?"

Her eyes danced across my face. "No reason. You just seem..."

I drew in a deep breath. "Discombobulated?"

She shook her head. "More like...happy."

I paused. "Happy?"

She smiled softly. "Yes. Happy, but you don't know what to do with it. You will, though, in time. Happiness always takes us by surprise but give it a couple of days. You'll know what to do next."

I ushered her out of the house and waved goodbye, then set my sights on Micah's room. Tonight was too much. It had been way too much, and what I needed was some sleep. I silently crept into my son's room and walked over to his bed, perching on the side of it.

And when he rolled toward me, I smoothed his hair out of his eyes.

"I love you so much," I whispered.

He turned back over, and I rubbed his back until soft snores fell from his lips. I'd never get over how comforting that sound was. How genuinely happy it made me to hear my son snoring lightly across the hallway. I'd gone through so many hurdles to have him. His birth alone was traumatic and raising him since—without a father figure around—had been nothing short of hell on earth. Every single possible ailment that could have plagued a young child befell my son. And every time I turned around, I was having to stay up into the wee hours of any given morning, taking on extra work just to afford his medical bills as an infant.

Thankfully, things had smoothed over in the end. But, for a time there, I thought we were going to be homeless.

"Sleep tight, Micah," I whispered.

And after bending over to kiss his cheek, I went to my bedroom. I made my way into the bathroom and started stripping myself of my party clothes. I laid my earrings out on the bathroom counter for Luna to collect whenever she came by next, and I washed off all of the makeup from my face. I slipped out of my dress and tossed it into the little trash can by the toilet, determined to burn it once I was in the right frame of mine.

Then, I kicked off my boots and ran myself a hot bath.

I poured in as many bubbles in as I could stand and eased my aching body into the hot water. I felt the evidence of my sins wash away with the water, tainting it instead of me. But, the second I closed my eyes, I saw Ryan there. Sitting with me in the tub. Offering to rub my shoulders and my feet before his hands slowly crept up my legs.

"Oh," I moaned softly.

My hand slid between my legs, and I softly parted my folds. The vision of Ryan alone did something to me, and my clit began pulsing furiously. I teased the tip of it, jumping as water continued to pour into the tub. And when the water gathered just above my breasts, I reached up with a quivering foot and turned off the faucet before plunging both of my hands between my legs.

"Shit," I hissed.

I heard his growling in the back of my mind as I pictured his form in front of me. His thick thighs, bared for the world, while his cock stood at attention. His balls hung low with need while he smirked at me from beneath that massive cowboy hat of his. I felt the phantom touches of his lips against my neck. Of his hands against my hips. My mouth heated with the memory of his tongue sliding against my own, commanding my body with one of its smallest organs.

"God, I can't wait to know what your tongue feels like here," I gasped.

I circled my clit faster as I threw my right leg over the edge of the tub. Water sprinkled onto the tiled flooring as I bucked against my hands, my fingers trying pathetically to fill me. They didn't amount to how Ryan felt. Not by a longshot. His thick girth was something I'd never forget, and as I worked my clit with a feverish passion, I found myself hoping and praying we'd meet again. Hopefully, for a much longer time than tonight.

"Ryan! Oh! Just like that. Oh, fuck, just like *that*."

My head fell back against the tub, and my nipples puckered almost painfully as my body threw itself over the edge again. Water lapped at my neck, caressing me with bubbles as I squeezed my eyes shut. Sounds of Ryan orgasming echoed off the corners of my mind, spiraling me into a moment of ecstasy where I could have begged for him, had he been there.

But, as I collapsed beneath the water of the bath—using it to rip me from my trance—I found myself alone...again.

Just like I always was.

I came up for air and unplugged the tub. I needed to rid Ryan from my mind. I needed to piece myself together, grow up, and stop indulging in some schoolyard crush. I had too many things on my plate to worry about. I had a business that I needed to make work. I had a child who required all of the free attention I could give him. And the last thing I needed was to get tangled up with a man like Ryan.

A handsome, strong, commanding man like him.

Who probably wanted more than I could give him, anyway.

Maybe you should ask instead of assuming.

"I'm going to find a way to mute you one of these days," I hissed.

I climbed out of the bath and dried off. Then, I slung my robe around my body. I tied off a bow around my waist and padded into the kitchen before I started making myself a cup of hot apple cider. I didn't need the caffeine that came with coffee, but I needed something warm to help lull me to sleep. And after filling my favorite rainbow-colored mug with the piping hot liquid, I settled into the recliner in the living room before turning on some mindless television.

I sipped my drink and watched a muted episode of *Golden Girls,* but every once in a while, my eyes found their way out the window. I glanced off toward the forest where I knew the cobblestone pathway was, and I eagerly watched for Ryan. Maybe he'd come after me. Or, maybe he'd go get comfortable and then pop by to hang out. The more I watched, though, the more it became abundantly clear to me.

I wanted to see Ryan again.

Much sooner, rather than much later.

11

Ryan

The first thing I felt was the heartburn. It was like someone was searing a hole into my chest from the inside out. I swallowed, and the bitter, sour taste left much to be desired until I drew in a deep breath. "Fuck," I grunted.

I rolled over onto my side and spit onto the floor. It had been a long-ass time since I'd drunk that much, but the faint smell of Ellie still on my skin brought the evening rushing back. I licked my lips and remembered how lovely her tongue had tasted. I rolled onto my back again and envisioned what it might feel like to have her bouncing above me while I played with her luxurious tits.

I grinned as I raised myself up out of bed.

Then, I dragged my lazy ass into a cold shower.

My hangover quickly drifted off as I let the water wash away the rest of my sins. I let some of the water pour into my mouth, and I swished it around before spitting it back out onto my feet. I did that a few times to rid my mouth of the disgusting aftertaste of stale beer and open-mouthed snoring. Then, I swallowed a couple of mouthfuls before washing myself down.

And the entire time, I thought of Ellie.

I wondered what she was doing and how she was feeling. She had kept up with me, drink for drink, so surely she had to feel as shitty as I did. Was she taking a shower right now? Was she still asleep? Was she already up and at work?

It's Saturday, of course, she's not at work.

As much as I hated to wash her off my skin, I had to pull myself together. I had my first video interview with surrogates just before lunchtime, and I needed to look as presentable as possible. I was still on the fence about whether or not this was the right avenue for me, but it couldn't hurt to speak with women who had already gone through this with another person.

After cleaning myself up, I picked out my best suit to put on for the video calls.

I brewed myself a cup of hot coffee before straightening my tie. Even though they wouldn't see me from the chest down, I still wanted to dress as if I were meeting them in person. After all, one of these women would—potentially— give me the one thing I couldn't give myself. And the least I could do was dress up and make them feel like this was important while speaking with me.

Then, I sat at my small desk in the corner by the window to get some sunshine.

"Come on, Ryan, no need to be nervous," I said breathlessly.

I choked down the black coffee, and it washed away the remainder of my hangover. I popped two pills for a headache just in case my body felt like betraying me, and as I reached for a snack in the mini-fridge I kept by my desk, my laptop started to ring.

So, I poised myself before answering it. "Good morning, Miss Delacour."

A pretty little redhead smiled back at me. "Good morning, Mr. Remington. How are you?"

I nodded. "I'm well and yourself?"

Her smile grew. "I'm just great."

"Before we get started, have you signed the NDA I sent to you?"

She held up a paper copy. "I have a paper copy for myself, but you should have an electronically signed one in your email."

I checked my phone and, sure enough, the signed NDA was there. Along with four others, two of which I'd speak with right after her.

"I appreciate it, as I'm sure you understand this matter is a sensitive one," I said.

She shrugged as she put down the NDA. "It's pretty

commonplace, especially with men like yourself, but I totally understand."

I nodded. "I'm glad that you do. So, I'll be upfront. I'm a bit lost as to how something like this works. But why don't you start by telling me a little about yourself?"

She leaned back in her chair. "Well, I have a master's in education. I'm a mathematics professor at Southern Methodist."

"How long have you been working there?"

"This is my fifth year teaching at the college. My husband is an English professor there as well."

My eyebrows rose. "So, you're married, but your husband is okay with you being a surrogate?"

She snickered. "That does strike many as odd, but yes, he's completely okay with it."

"If you don't mind my asking, how many surrogacies have you done?"

"Three, and none of them have had complications."

"What got you into this kind of thing in the first place?"

She giggled. "Honestly? It was my sister. She can't have children of her own, so I told her and her husband that if they really wanted kids, I'd carry their child for them."

My eyes widened. "Wow. That's incredible."

She smiled so hard that her eyes closed. "It kind of spiraled from there, I guess. I've got two kids of my own, and I always loved being pregnant. My sister was my first surrogacy, then after many conversations with my husband, I signed up for the surrogacy list here in Texas. The other two I've done have been from that list."

The woman seemed pleasant enough, but there was something about her that I couldn't place. She was kind, sure, and very forthcoming with my questions. But, there wasn't that spark of trust there that Dr. Valconie said most people talked about.

So, I thanked her for the interview and silently crossed her off my list.

After hers, the next video conference was nice enough, but she wasn't as willing to answer my questions. She actually took offense to a couple of them, and I figured if she couldn't handle a simple interview, then she certainly couldn't handle my hovering over her while she was pregnant. So, I quickly moved on to the last meeting for my day.

And the cutest blonde I'd ever seen popped up on the screen. "Mr. Remington! Good afternoon. My name's Leslie."

I nodded. "Good to meet you."

"You, too."

"So, why don't you tell me a bit about yourself? What makes Leslie, Leslie?"

She giggled. "Well, I'm a stay-at-home-mother. I've got two twin girls who are seven years old, and they are a handful."

I chuckled. "I can only imagine."

"And before you ask, I've only done surrogacy one other time, but things went very well. Very few complications during birth, a very healthy baby as a byproduct, and I didn't experience any sort of PPD or anything like that."

I blinked. "PPD?"

"Post-partum depression? It's common in surrogates, especially when they carry a child they then don't get to hold. But, I never experienced that. I had ways of combatting the attachment that usually comes with my body growing children."

"That's very good to know. You said very few complications, though. Were there some when you gave birth?"

She shrugged. "They had to use one of those head vacuums to get the baby out, but that was because the baby was absolutely gigantic. My girls were around five or so pounds each, but this one child was them put together."

My jaw dropped open. "You shoved out a ten-pound child naturally?"

"Oh, trust me, I was drugged to the high heavens. But, other than a tear that required three little stitches and that head vacuum, things were just fine."

I shook my head. "You women are powerhouses, you know that?"

She barked with laughter. "Someone has to be, especially when the men get sick."

It was less like a formal interview with Leslie and more like I'd been speaking with a long-lost friend. And not only was she forthcoming with information, but she also seemed happy to offer up more than I asked. I mean, the woman was married, down to earth, she'd already done this surrogacy thing once so we both weren't going in blind, and she didn't take offense to any of my prodding questions.

I like her. "So, hypothetically speaking for a second, what might come after this?"

She leaned back in her chair. "Well, that all depends. Do you have a woman you're having a child with, or is it just you?"

"Just me."

She licked her lips. "Well, you can go about it a few ways: there are egg donation centers just like sperm donation centers where you can go in and choose a set of eggs you wish to incubate."

"I didn't even know those existed. That's probably the route I'll go."

She giggled. "Good, because I don't think my husband would like one of the other routes."

"What do you mean?"

She leaned forward. "There are some women in the surrogacy arena that'll charge extra for using her own eggs."

I blinked. "Like, me have a child with you specifically?"

She leaned back a bit. "Yup."

"Uh, no offense to you or anything, but no. That seems a bit weird."

She laughed so hard, she snorted. "Right? I mean, whatever makes them money, but I couldn't do it. I mean, that's my child out there that I don't get to raise. How screwed up is that?"

I paused. "Is there another option besides those two? You made it seem like there were."

"Oh, of course! The other popular option is for you to have a woman you *do* want to have a child with, then you take your sperm and her egg and create an embryo that's then implanted into my uterus. I grow your child, shove it out, and that child is full-on the two of you, DNA and all."

"I mean, I like that idea, but I kind of need a woman to make that part happen."

She snickered. "Well, that's why there are those egg donation centers. They're very professional, very clean, and very discreet as well. You wouldn't have any problem there."

I sighed. "Well, you've been an absolute delight to speak with, Leslie."

"And you as well, Mr. Remington. However, there's one more thing you should know about me before you make any sort of a decision."

I quirked an eyebrow. "Is this where you tell me you secretly want to have my child but you don't want to say anything about it?"

She giggled profusely. "Sorry to burst your bubble, but my heart lies only with my husband. But, I just want you to know that—with me, at least—you won't have to worry about buying formula. I'm practically a milk cow after giving birth, so I'll pump and give you breast milk for your child through its first year of life."

I blinked. "Seriously? You do that?"

She nodded. "Oh, yeah. I'd give you control over my diet, so I'm not ingesting anything you don't want your baby ingesting, and I'd pump on a regular basis and hand it over to you. And if you need recommendations for burp-resistant bottles, I'm your gal. I've tried everything on the market when it came to my girls, and I know which ones work best."

I shook my head. "I really like you, you know that?"

She placed her hand over her heart. "Awww, that's so kind of you to say! Thank you!"

I clicked my tongue. "I don't want to say anything for certain yet because I've got a couple more interviews to do tomorrow, but just keep an eye on your email come next week, okay?"

She nodded. "Sir, yes, sir!"

I chuckled. "It was very nice meeting you, Leslie."

"And you as well, Mr. Remington."

"Please, call me Ryan."

She smiled. "Ryan, it is. Until we speak again, Ryan."

"Until we speak again, Leslie."

Just as I got off the video call with the woman who would probably be my surrogate, a knock came at the door. It made me jump a bit, seeing as the knock was pretty hard, and my heart stopped in my chest.

Maybe it's Ellie. "Who is it?"

A loud thud sounded again. "Dude, are you gonna open this door or what?"

Boone's voice sounded through the door before Wyatt spoke up as well. "Seriously, we bring lunch and more coffee. And it's getting heavy out here."

I pushed myself away from my desk and walked over to

the door. And when I opened it, I saw both of my brothers with cockeyed sunglasses on their faces.

I chuckled. "Rough night?"

Boone charged into the room. "Ugh, get out of the way."

Wyatt shoved the food and coffees into my arms. "I call the bed."

"No, I call the bed."

"Not if I get there first."

My brothers launched themselves onto my queen-size bed as I kicked the door closed. I walked the food over to my little kitchenette and started divvying everything up. They were groaning and whining as if they had come down with the flu or some shit, and it reminded me of the conversation I had just had with Leslie.

I started chuckling to myself before Wyatt spoke up. "The fuck's so funny?"

I peeked over at them. "You two sound like sick kids."

Boone groaned. "Shut up and feed me food."

Wyatt sighed. "How are you okay from last night?"

I turned toward them with a plate of food in each hand. "Because I know how to deal with hangovers. Something you guys apparently haven't figured out yet. Now, sit up and eat. And don't spill shit on my bed."

Boone took his plate from me. "I know why he doesn't feel like shit."

Wyatt set his plate in his lap. "Why's that?"

Boone snickered. "Because he spent his entire night with Eeeeeeh-llie last night."

Wyatt spoke with his mouthful. "You know, I saw y'all tearin' it up on the dance floor. She's a pretty good dancer."

I leaned against the counter and picked at my food. "Yeah, after I taught her. You know she didn't even know how to two-step?"

Boone swallowed hard. "Blasphemy."

Wyatt chugged his coffee. "Anyone drunk enough can two-step."

I chuckled. "Amen to that."

Boone grinned up at me. "So, where did you two get off to once you stumbled out of the barn? And don't act like it didn't happen because I watched the whole thing."

I blinked. "What were you doing, stalking us or some shit?"

Boone shrugged. "Doesn't matter. All I know is that you two never came back."

Wyatt paused. "Oh, shit. Did you get with Ellie?"

I shot him a look as the lie poured from my lips. "If you really want to know, I helped Ellie get back to her guesthouse. She was just as drunk as I was, and I didn't feel comfortable with her navigating the pathway back to her place after shoving drinks down her throat all night."

Boone narrowed his eyes. "And you stayed with her there, right?"

I blinked. "She had a babysitter there with her kid, you idiot."

Wyatt took a big bite of his wrap. "Wouldn't have stopped me."

My eyes widened. "Since when did you go from 'business, business, business' to 'manwhore, manwhore, manwhore'?"

He peeked up at me. "I learned from the best, that's how. And I can turn off work on the weekends if I need to, jackass."

I rolled my eyes. "Could've fooled me."

Boone interjected, "So, let me get this straight: this girl you've been crushing on—and don't you dare deny it—gets drunk with you and dances all night. Leaves with you. Walks with you back to her place, and you don't fucking stay?"

Wyatt pointed at me. "I call bullshit."

Boone nodded. "Me, too."

I took a sip of my coffee. "I don't care what you *call*, I know the truth whether you want to believe it or not."

Boone scoffed. "I'll figure out what really happened sooner or later."

Wyatt finished off his food. "I, for one, think it's good that he didn't let himself get distracted with some girl. I mean, don't get me wrong, Ellie's pretty and all. But, we've got a shitshow with this company right now that we have to get under control, and the last thing any of us need is a distraction in our lives."

Boone shrugged. "Whatever."

I turned my attention to the rest of my food and tried to stuff down my guilty feelings. I felt like shit for lying to my brothers about things with Ellie, but the last thing I needed was them sinking their teeth into something that wasn't theirs to devour. I'd lost count at the number of possible relationships they had ruined for me simply because they jumped the gun with shit. I mean, it wasn't like I wanted to be single. I was simply single because my brothers were fucking wolves when it came to grilling any woman who came into my life.

They said they were trying to save me from gold-diggers and honey-rakers.

But, I thought they were just jealous that women threw themselves at me and not them.

"So, we gonna talk about hiring for these last few positions at the headquarters? Or no?" Wyatt asked.

I paused. "Didn't you just say—?"

He stood to his feet. "When I feel like shit, I'll say anything to get someone to shut up. So, when do we want to start picking through resumes?"

And I figured this distraction was as good as any.

Especially now that I had found a really good candidate for my surrogacy vision.

12

Ellie

"Ellie's Blacksmithing, this is Ellie speaking."

The voice on the other end sounded cheerier than I needed for ten in the morning after dousing myself in Tylenol to get rid of my hangover.

"Ellie! Hi there! It's Rita. Remember me?"

I paused. "Rita Riley?"

"Yes! Hi. I hope I'm not bothering you? Your website said you have truncated Saturday hours."

I paused the email I was typing up. "Yes, I do. It's mostly office hours for me to catch up on paperwork and such, but I also take appointments and things like that on Saturdays."

"Fantastic, do you have any appointments available for today?"

I blinked. "For another project?"

She laughed. "Yes, silly. For another project. My husband loves this wrought-iron railing you made and installed for our master suite balcony. He was wondering if you could craft one just like it for our staircase? You know, to match?"

I had to take a second and rejoice in my head. I screamed and imagined myself standing up to dance. Tears rushed my eyes as I pushed away from my laptop, and I raced for the coffee pot, trying to pour myself a mug in order to calm my nerves.

Finally, I had my first recurring customer.

"Ellie?"

I choked down the lukewarm coffee. "Yes, my apologies. Just pulling up my schedule. I've got an available appointment right before lunch and right after lunch. Which would you prefer?"

"Before, definitely. The sooner, the better."

I smiled. "Wonderful. I've got you on my schedule. I'll be there right at eleven!"

"I'm looking forward to it!"

The second I hung up the phone, I scrambled to finish my email. It was already ten-thirty, and I didn't have much time to make myself look presentable. I raced into the bathroom and splashed some water onto my face before I looked at myself in the mirror.

And when I saw my own smile, I squealed. "I did it! I did it! I can't believe I fucking did it!"

I dried off my face and threw my fists into the air. I rushed to get changed into a pair of jeans that weren't ripped and my nicest button-front shirt. Then, I snatched up my keys, slid my wallet into my back pocket, reached for my phone, and raced out the front door.

And I didn't get halfway up the road, though, before my cell rang again.

"Ellie's Blacksmithing, this is Ellie."

"Hello there, dear! It's Mrs. Schneider."

"Good morning, Mrs. Schneider, what can I do for you?"

She cleared her throat. "I was wondering if I could make a last-minute change to my order. And please, let me know if I can't."

I paused. "It depends on the change. I've already got most of the hand-twists done for your front porch railing, so we're at a point where we can't really change that specific order."

"No, no, no. That's fine. I was more or less looking to add to it?"

I tried not to get too excited as I sat at the stoplight. "What kind of additions?"

"Well, when I came by Thursday and saw just how wonderful things looked, it got me to thinking. Do you do other things besides railings and such?"

I nodded. "Oh, yes. I can do everything from railings and bed frames to picture frames. Even crafted and personalized silverware."

"Wait, really?"

"Mhm. Anything that can be made from metal, I can make."

"Oh, my goodness. That changes everything. Do you think you could stop by sometime today? I want to get an opinion on the vision I see for my son's bed frame."

Two recurring clients on the same day! "I'm heading to an appointment right now, but I can buzz by right after it. How does noon, sharp, sound?"

I heard her smile through the phone. "I'll make us up some food to have before I show you. Do you like sweet tea?"

I giggled. "Did Harry meet Sally?"

"Oh! Such a good movie. I knew I liked you. Yes, I'll see you promptly at noon."

"See you then, Mrs. Schneider."

My workday was a whirlwind of delights and new acquisitions. And by the time my first two recurring clients signed off on the quotes I had given them to start the jobs, I was seven-thousand dollars richer.

And I'd get half of that upfront within the next forty-eight hours.

I raced back to the stables to get started on the brothers' horseshoes for the upcoming championship rodeo, as well as the smaller rodeos that would take place between now and then. I always kept a shiny new pair on the walls for each of their horses and put new sets of shoes on the animals' feet after every rodeo. I always kept spares around, too, just in case something happened overnight while they were in the stables.

But, as I stuck the iron into the blazing hot furnace to

melt it down into the shapes I needed, a voice sounded behind me.

"I figured I'd find you here on a Saturday," Ryan said.

I snickered. "A growing business never takes a day off."

He pulled up a chair beside me. "You sound like my brothers."

I peeked over at him. "Then, your brothers are right."

"Boy, I'd never hear the end of it if I told them that shit."

I grinned. "Sometimes, it does need to be heard, though."

I felt his eyes on me. "So, how goes it?"

I furrowed my brow. "You've got something on your mind, don't you?"

He chuckled. "I guess I've always been easy to read."

I shrugged. "I'm good at reading people, though. Or, so I've been told."

He sighed. "It's just—I had to lie to my brothers this morning, and it's been eating me up ever since."

"Oh? What about?"

"About us and last night."

I slowly eased the liquid metal out of the furnace. "Oh."

"I'll wait until you're done pouring to continue."

I poured the metal into the horseshoe molds as quickly as I could before I put more metal back into the furnace to melt down.

"So, what did you have to lie about?" I asked.

Ryan scoffed. "They saw us leave the barn during the dance, and I told them I walked them back to your place."

COWBOY'S TEMPTING NEIGHBOR

Relief washed through my veins. "Well, it's none of their business what we got up to."

"I tell them everything, though. That's how we've always been."

I clicked my tongue. "Seeing as I don't give you permission to share that information, though, I would think you'd at least respect that."

He blinked. "Is there a reason why you're forbidding me to talk about it?"

I giggled. "That's kind of a harsh word. I just mean I don't like it when men go around boasting about how many times they got laid and what kind of freaky shit they did. It's gross and not very classy."

I was incredibly relieved that he had lied to his brothers because the last thing I needed was to have ridicule coming at me from all sides. Plus, I didn't need to be getting heavily involved with someone anyway since work was now taking off.

I needed to focus on this business now that I had proven that I could capture clients that came back.

Ryan finally broke the silence. "Well, if you don't want me talking about it, then I won't."

I nodded. "I appreciate that. And it's not that I want to hide it, but the last thing I need are the girls breathing down my neck and making this into more than what it is. My focus needs to be on this business, and I can't get sidetracked with that."

He stood. "Trust me, I totally get it."

I sighed. "I'm glad you do."

I removed the molten metal and poured it into the rest of the forms before setting it off to the side. Then, I peeled the first horseshoe out of the mold now that it had set enough with my tongs, and I started banging it into place. Sparks flew, and the metal quickly cooled, but I managed to get it in just the right shape.

But, when I put it off to the side and reached for another horseshoe, I found Ryan still staring at me.

"What?" I asked.

He narrowed his eyes. "Something happened today, didn't it?"

I cocked my head. "With what?"

He wiggled his finger in front of him. "With this, with the business. Something happened today, didn't it?"

I grinned. "I have my first two recurring clients."

His jaw dropped open. "Ellie, that's amazing! Congratulations!"

I started banging away. "I know, right? I mean, it took me long enough to do it, but I went from not having any at all to having two back to back! Ugh, it feels so good."

"They gonna pay you well?"

I snorted. "While it's kind of uncouth to talk about pay, I will say that this will be my biggest pay month since starting this up. And that's just with the down payments."

He clapped his hands and rubbed them together. "This calls for a celebration."

I shook my head. "Oh, no. I've got way too much work to do now that I have two new projects in my lap."

"Come on, Ellie. You can spare a dinner tonight so that we can go out and celebrate."

I placed the horseshoe off to the side and paused. "Dinner? Tonight?"

He nodded. "Yeah! Why not? We could even make it an early dinner so you can get back to Micah before he goes to bed. What's his bedtime?"

There he goes, being a gentleman again. "Uh, I usually get him down around eight or so."

He held out his arms. "Great. I'll take you out for dinner around five, you'll be back before seven, and you've got time to wind down and hang out with the little man before he goes to sleep."

I peeled another horseshoe out of its mold. "I don't know..."

"My treat, and if you want to invite the girls, you're more than welcome to. The more, the merrier."

I started hammering the horseshoe into place. "I can invite the girls?"

"Yep. If you'd like them to come. The guys are all busy tonight, though. Family night and all that."

Which means the girls won't be available. "Well, I'll ask them and see what they think, but it'll probably just be the two of us tonight."

He smirked. "So, is that a 'yes' to dinner?"

I held his gaze with my own. "Yes, okay. You can pick me

up around five. I just have to finish up these shoes, and then I can grab a quick shower."

And the smile that spread across his face made me weak in my knees. I was having dinner out tonight. With Ryan. The hottest guy I'd ever hooked up with.

Shit, I really need another dress.

❧ 13 ❧

Ryan

I chuckled when Ellie opened the door. "Well, well, well, would you look at those boots."

She looked down at them. "Too much?"

I crooked my finger underneath her chin and pulled her gaze up to mine. "I think a shined pair of boots is a wonderful thing. They look great on you."

She smiled softly. "Wonderful. So, where are we off to for dinner?"

It took all I had to pull away from her instead of kissing that pair of ruby lips. "How does barbecue sound?"

She groaned. "That sounds heavenly. Drown it all down with some sweet tea and I'm a happy camper."

I offered her my arm. "Anything you want. It's your day to celebrate."

Escorting Ellie to Rick's BBQ and Pies should've been the highlight of my day. Sitting across from a beautiful woman while she ordered a plate that challenged my own should've made my heart melt in her presence. Hell, even the way she smiled and laughed at my jokes should've had me ecstatic simply to be in her company.

It wasn't any of that, though, that attracted me to her. The thing that sucked me in the most was how strong of a woman she was. "I'm not sure if I could ever do what you do, you know," I said.

Ellie took a sip of her tea. "What do you mean?"

I shrugged. "I mean, you have a two-year-old, and you're building this business from the ground up. You moved into an area you weren't familiar with, somehow managed to plant roots, you negotiated an amazing arrangement with my half-brothers you're currently working on, and somehow you still have time to laugh and smile and forget about things. I just don't get it."

She smiled softly. "You gotta do whatcha gotta do sometimes, you know? No one ever knows how strong they are until they're forced to be such."

I cocked my head. "What forced you to buckle down and be strong?"

Her eyes moved away from mine, and I knew I'd struck a nerve. It made me so upset that something had happened to this girl. Something that wasn't the kind of good she deserved. But, I was here to take her mind off things, to celebrate her victories, not to revel or dwell in her pitfalls.

So, I raised my glass of sweet tea. "To Ellie and her business, may it be as successful as she deserves."

Her smile immediately came back as she clinked her glass with mine. "Hear, hear."

I winked at her. "Make sure you save room for dessert. There's a reason this place is called Rick's BBQ *and* Pies."

She hummed as she set her tea down. "Please tell me they have pecan pie year-round."

"What kind of Texas barbecue place would it be if they didn't?"

As we placed our pie and coffee orders, I found myself wanting to ask about her son. I wanted to know about Micah and who his father was. I wanted to know where they came from and how she had grown up. But, something in the pit of my gut told me not to press those topics. Besides, if she wanted to speak with me about her past, she would in her own time. Though, I was curious as to why a beautiful, intelligent, capable woman such as herself was single.

Maybe it's because she's a mom, too.

"Is your family's petrol company how you saw your future panning out?" she asked.

Her voice pulled me from my trance. "As shocking as this is to say, no."

She giggled. "What did you want to be before all of that came about?"

"Honestly? A fireman."

She smiled. "Every little boy's dream."

I took a massive bite of my pie. "Oh, God. This is fantastic. How's yours?"

She picked up her fork. "Guess I should try it instead of staring at the man in front of me, huh?"

Our eyes met. "I suppose you should."

She watched me the entire time she took a bite of her pecan pie, and when her eyes rolled back, I felt my jeans tightening around my hips. She moaned as it melted against the tip of her tongue like all of their pies did to me, and I swear to fuck, I wanted to stuff her mouth full while she moaned around my dick. She sat back in her chair and savored it, chewing slowly and sticking out that tongue of hers to lick the small piece of crust residue off her lower lip.

Dammit, does she know what she's doing to me?

Ellie's eyes opened. "All right, you need to take a bite of this so I can justify taking a bite of your cherry pie. Because it looks phenomenal."

I barked with laughter. "On the count of three."

"Ready?"

I nodded. "Three!"

We both reached over the table and quickly dove into each other's pies. I felt her hair tickling my neck as she pressed her forehead against my shoulder, humming with delight as she took a bite of my pie. I stuffed my face with a massive bite of her pecan pie, and I could have sank to the floor in weakness the damned thing was so good.

And when we both flopped down into our seats, Ellie eyed me carefully.

"All in favor of a second dessert?" she asked.

I raised my hand as quickly as I could. "Waitress? We're ready for some more pie!"

Everyone in the small barbecue house chuckled at us as our waitress held her finger up in the air. And as Ellie perused the dessert menus they kept propped up on the tables, I couldn't take my eyes off her. The way her natural waves made her blond hair look wild. The way her deep, sea-blue eyes seemed to draw me in even if she wasn't looking directly at me. I couldn't take my eyes off her. She was an absolutely beautiful woman.

And before I knew it, I blurted out a question I had no right in asking. "Do you want more children someday?"

Her eyes froze on the menu. "What was that?"

I cleared my throat. "I was just wondering because I've seen you from afar with Micah, and you're so good with him. I know I want a big family someday, and I was just curious as to whether or not you saw yourself in a big family or anything like that."

Our waitress finally approached us. "Now, what can I get the happy couple?"

Ellie slid the menu off to the side. "Actually, I think I'll pass on the second dessert."

I blinked. "Are you sure? Because their blueberry pie is outstanding."

The waitress winked at me. "Our blueberry pie put us on the map!"

Ellie's eyes wouldn't meet mine. "Just some more coffee is fine, thank you."

"And for you, sugar?" the waitress asked.

I felt like an idiot for beckoning her over, so I ordered anyway. "I'll take a slice of that blueberry pie to go, thank you."

Ellie sighed. "You don't have to do that. I just didn't expect the question, that's all."

I leaned forward as the waitress walked away. "I'm sorry if that question was too prying or anything like that."

"It's not that."

Something passed behind her eyes, but it happened so quickly that I couldn't do anything but brush it off. I was concerned that she'd pull even further away from me if I asked her about it.

And I definitely didn't want that to happen.

"Ellie?" I asked.

Her eyes finally met mine. "Yep?"

I smiled softly. "I'm really proud of you and what you've accomplished."

Her eyes twinkled again. "Seriously?"

I nodded. "Seriously. Not everyone can do what you do. There are single mothers out there day in and day out, struggling to make ends meet. Struggling to find their worth after being shit on and left. You're kicking ass and taking names, and I know you're only going to keep going up from here."

She smiled, and I felt the sincerity of it radiating like the summer sun. "I really appreciate that, Ryan. Thank you."

I love it when you say my name. "You're more than welcome."

Our waitress returned. "One blueberry pie, to go, and one coffee. I got it to-go as well, just in case. I hope that's okay?"

Ellie looked up and nodded. "That's perfect, actually. Thank you."

Our waitress beamed. "Now, here's your ticket. Ain't no rush, but you can pay at the register when ya leave. Thanks for comin' by and see in' me!"

I scooped up the check. "Thank you for having us. It was wonderful."

Ellie nodded vigorously. "Yes, it was fantastic. Thank you."

Our bubbly little waitress traipsed off with her auburn curls bouncing around her shoulders. I gestured for Ellie to take as long as she wanted while I went and paid the bill. Then, I offered her my arm and escorted her to my truck. We rode back to the ranch in silence, but I wasn't sure if the silence was good. I mean, it didn't seem tense, but it also didn't seem giddy or cheerful.

Not like it had been while we drove to the restaurant.

"Ellie, if I said anything that made you—"

She whipped her head around as my truck came to a stop. "It's not you. It's me."

I blinked. "*Oh*...kay?"

She sighed. "Yes, you struck a nerve that I'm not prepared to talk about yet. But, you couldn't have possibly known. It's not your fault."

I nodded softly. "Is there anything I can do to make you smile before you head on in?"

She peered out the window. "Ah, we're already here."

I snickered. "I mean, I could have falsely assumed things and taken you back to my loft. But, something tells me you wouldn't have liked that."

She looked up at me. "I suppose I could invite you in, if I really wanted to."

My cock lurched against my jeans. "I suppose you could."

Our eyes held each other's, and I felt my heart slam against my chest. There was pain behind Ellie's gaze. Pain she didn't deserve to feel. And suddenly, I was ready to tear open her past and figure out what—or who—had hurt her so I could do everything in my power to fix it.

She's not a damsel in distress. She doesn't need saving.

"Ryan?" Ellie asked.

I cleared my throat. "Sorry, yes. What did you say?"

She searched my eyes. "Wasn't important."

I'm a fucking idiot. "It's important to me. Why don't we go inside and—?"

She held her hand out for me to shake. "Thank you for a wonderful celebratory dinner. I really enjoyed myself."

I looked down at her hand. "I did, too."

She wiggled her fingers. "Not a handshaking kind of person?"

Not with someone like you. "Just feels a bit... formal."

She pulled her hand back. "Well, thank you for driving. I'm not sure I could've concentrated with this full stomach."

My eyes found hers. "Are you sure you don't want me to escort you inside?"

She swallowed hard. "I think that's for the best, yes."

And as she slipped out of my truck without another word spoken, the sting of her words settled against my soul. *For the best?* She thought us being apart was for the best? Did she not have fun like I had tonight? Did she really not enjoy dinner?

Was it something I said?

No matter the reason, though, I waited until she was safely inside before I pulled away. I turned my truck around and headed in the direction of the stables, ready to strip down and shower this failure of an evening off my skin. Yeah, all guys got rejected every once in a while. Even the infamous Will Remington before Sadie had locked him down tight as a whistle.

But, this one hurt a little deeper than most.

And I had no fucking clue as to why.

🌿 14 🌿

Ellie

I had enough time to shower and get myself into comfortable clothes before Mrs. Weatherford dropped off Micah. I scooped my sweet little boy into my arms and held him close, sniffing the wonderful scent of his scalp. I thanked Mrs. Weatherford with a soft nod before she closed my front door, and I settled into my rocker recliner as my son buried his face into the crook of my neck.

And as I let out a heavy sigh, I started rocking my little boy in my arms.

"You are my Micah, my only Micah," I said softly, "you make me happy when skies are gray."

I let my eyes fall closed as I cradled him against my chest like I used to do whenever he was an infant. I remembered back to the night when I had told my ex that I was pregnant and how he had stormed out on me before effectively blocking my number. That night, I had cradled my seven-week-old embryo in the palms of my hands against my stomach while rocking in a rocking chair, hoping and praying that I'd be able to create a life from the ashes that laid at my feet.

But, every time I seemed to take two steps forward, there was always a massive step that knocked me back a few pegs.

...and I was just curious as to whether or not you saw yourself in a big family or anything like that.

"At least now I can write him off," I murmured to myself.

Now that I knew I could never give him what he wanted out of his life, it seemed like a no-brainer. I now had the capability of writing Ryan off as quickly as he'd come rushing into my world, and I no longer had to trip and stumble over myself just to be in his presence.

But, the idea of not having Ryan around made me sad. And I found myself blinking back tears as my son snored softly against my skin.

"I love you so much, Micah," I whispered.

I kissed the side of his head before standing to my feet. I walked him gingerly into his bedroom to put him into bed, watching as he spread out with his arms and legs. He made it so easy for me to undress him while he was half-asleep, and I took in as much of the moment as possible. With the kinds of complications I dealt with daily now, I'd never experience this again with another child. I'd never experience the joy of having a helpless child in my arms and feeding it with my own body. I'd never experience the wonders of shopping for clothes that could fit into the palms of both of my hands. I'd never even get to experience what it might be like to tell a man I was pregnant and have him stay instead of leave.

"I'm going to give you the world on a platter," I whispered as I slid my sleeping son into his pajamas. "Just you wait."

After sliding his favorite blankie up his body and giving him a stuffed animal Sadie purchased for him the day he was born, I eased myself out of his bedroom. I had a headache from hell and tears that needed to be shed lest I feel every ounce of emotionally hungover in the morning. And the last thing I needed on my one day off was a fucking migraine to deal with.

But, a rapid knock at my front door filled the space around me.

"Shit, shit, shit, shit, shit," I hissed.

I darted for the door and reached for the knob, preparing myself for the emergency on the other end. I'd only ever heard that knock one other time, and it was when Will came to get me because Sadie had to be rushed to the hospital. My heart plummeted to my toes as I ripped open the door, expecting yet another hospital visit to come falling into my lap.

Except it wasn't any of the girls on the other side.

It was Ryan.

I panted softly. "What the hell?"

He furrowed his brow. "Ellie."

I blinked. "What are you doing here? What's wrong?"

Before I could get another word out of my mouth, his lips covered mine. His hands cupped my cheeks, and his body pushed me inside while his tongue invaded the roof of my mouth. The tips of my teeth. The swell of my own tongue as they wrapped together in a joyous chorus that left me wanting more. I kicked the front door closed with my foot before Ryan spun me around. He pinned me to the wall behind me before sliding my hands above my head.

He held them there with only one of his before our kiss ended.

And when my gaze found his stare, I saw his desire for me. "More," I whispered.

His lips attacked my neck, causing me to moan softly as he suckled against my pulse point. His knee pressed between my legs, parting them as the heat of my pussy fell against his thigh. I felt myself caving to him in ways I didn't need to be. He was the kind of man I wanted to get attached to. The kind of man I wanted to attach to me in return. But, I knew it would only end in disappointment when he figured everything out.

"All I want is you," he growled against my collarbone.

His voice rattled my ribcage as I drew in a soft breath. "Then take me, Ryan."

And that was all I had to say for him to grip my ass cheeks and hoist me against his body.

❧ 15 ❧

Ryan

I walked her down the hallway as my lips peppered kisses along her delicate, exposed skin. Her legs locked around my waist as I padded into her room, kicking the door closed behind me. She giggled as she gripped my hair. I laid her against the mattress as her legs fell away from my body. And as I kissed down the valley of her clothed breasts, only one thing was for certain in my mind. Tonight, I'd have Ellie the way I had wanted to have her at the dance.

"Ryan," she whispered.

I slid my hands up her shirt and quickly slipped it over her head. Her bouncing breasts, puckered and ready for my tongue, looked positively scrumptious as I bent over to have a taste. She undulated against me, raking those hips against my stiffening cock as the heat of her pussy poured through her panties. And as I lapped at her nipples, her hands slid through my hair.

"Lower. Lower, please," she begged.

I growled as I sank to my knees. I kissed down Ellie's stomach and slid her pants off her body. I kissed along where her hip bones would have been, reveling in the feeling of her bucking and moaning and shivering against me. I smelled her pussy as I slid my nose softly down the inside of her thigh. I kissed up to the crevice of where her leg met her wetness, teasing her with the tip of my tongue.

"Ryan, come on," she groaned.

And after a bit of a chuckle, I slid her underwear to the side.

"Oh, fuck," she hissed.

I pressed my tongue between her folds, and the taste of her washed over me like the waves of an angry ocean. Her juices coated my cheeks as I pressed myself tightly against her, feeling her legs sliding over my shoulders. I lapped slowly at her clit, her entrance pulsing with every stroke of my salivating tongue.

But, it wasn't until I pressed two fingers deep inside of her that I felt her unraveling.

"Oh, shit. Oh, fuck. Ryan, please. Please, you feel—so, so good."

I flattened my tongue against her pussy and pumped my

fingers furiously inside of her. She wiggled against the mattress, her legs falling weak against my shoulders. Her juices poured over my hand. I felt her dripping down my chin and coating my neck, marking me in the only way she could. I growled deeply against her swollen clit as she whimpered the sweetest, most amazing set of words to ever cross my ears.

And with those words, I leaked against my pants.

"I can't wait for you to fill me. Please, let me come."

I sucked her clit between my lips and watched her back arch. Her skin flushed a deep shade of crimson red that made me feel more amazing and more alive than ever before as I simply witnessed it. Her nipples puckered into tighter peaks as her tits bounced for my viewing pleasure. And when her walls clenched around my fingers, I felt something inside me pop.

I sprang to my feet as her orgasm wound down and pulled out my cock, ready to stuff her full in every way she wished.

"Legs up," I commanded.

She groaned as her shaking legs slowly raised themselves into the air. I moved between them, letting her settle her calves against my strong shoulders as I guided myself to her entrance. She was still pulsing as I eased myself inside of her tight warmth. She gripped my dick with everything she had as her jaw unhinged, and her eyes flung themselves open.

And when her hands wrapped around my wrists, I bent her in half.

Feeling the last of me slide deeply into her body.

"Holy shit," she choked out.

I grinned. "You better hold on for the ride, sweet girl."

I pounded against her, watching as her face contorted with effervescent pleasure. This was what I had wanted the first time we had hooked up. This was what I needed after a long fucking day of dealing with family and putting up with business bullshit. Her moisture ran down my balls as they smacked against her wet ass crack. I wiggled out of her grip and pinned her arms over her head, watching as she laid there, helpless to my assault.

Then, I felt my hips shuttering.

"Come for me," she begged.

My lips dropped to hers as my tongue invaded her mouth. I covered her with my body as her legs slid off my shoulders, my cock buried deep inside of her quivering walls. She locked her ankles and pulled me deeper, our tongues dancing the tango they were quickly becoming familiar with. And as I rutted against her like a fucking wild animal, I felt my balls pull up quickly into my body.

"That's it," she whispered against my lips, "come for me, Ryan. Let go."

My jaw shivered as my orgasm crashed over my body. Ellie's back arched, pressing her heart against my own as the two of us spiraled down the rabbit hole, our bodies locked together. Our juices intermingled. Our lips touching. Our tongues dancing.

It was more than I could bear.

And the second my cock started coating her walls, my knees gave out.

"I gotcha. Rest against me," Ellie said breathlessly.

My face pressed into the crook of her neck as nothing short of euphoria swept over my body. It felt like the entire world was tilting off its axis at the weight of the earthquake that came crashing down against my body. Never had I ever experienced such pleasure with someone. Never had an orgasm rocked me the way that one did.

And as I kissed her neck over and over, I felt our intermingled arousal leaking onto her sheets. "Sorry for the mess," I murmured.

She giggled. "It's okay. I'll be fine."

I sighed. "You're amazing."

She started running her fingers through my hair. "Is this the part where I ask you how your day's been?"

The two of us shared a little laugh at her question. But it was a fair question.

"Is that something you want to know about?" I asked as I lifted my head.

She gazed into my eyes. "If you want to talk about it, sure."

My cock was still sheathed inside of her as I propped myself up onto my elbows, hovering above her. "Well, I had a couple more video conferences that I had to get through today."

"Nice, nice. Anything else you had to do?"

I shrugged. "Some paperwork. A couple of calls to different board members. I made a trip out to the new headquarters to look through a stack of resumes so we can fill the rest of the jobs open for that building."

"Sounds like you had a productive day."

I grinned. "Very. How was yours?"

She shrugged. "Eh, it was okay."

I quirked an eyebrow. "Just okay?"

She nodded. "Yeah. Just okay."

I whistled lowly. "Wow, you really make a man work for it, don't you?"

She barked with laughter before clapping her hand over her mouth, and I tried to shush her in between my own stifled chuckles. Our foreheads fell together as we giggled like little school-aged children with their first crushes, and my heart felt at peace. My soul felt at home. There was something about this woman that I couldn't shake, and for the life of me, I couldn't figure out what it was.

But I really liked it.

Don't forget about the video meetings you had today.

"Ryan? You okay?" Ellie asked.

I slowly leaned up and let my cock fall from between her legs. The meetings. I'd had more video conferences with possible surrogates earlier that morning. And being on the brink of taking that major step in my life, it wouldn't be fair to bring her into that kind of scenario. I mean, Ellie already had a kid! And the last thing she needed to be doing while trying to build her business was juggling an older man who was living out some fantasy I couldn't have because I had prioritized business and work over everything else in my life for more years than I should have.

"Ryan. Look at me," Ellie said.

Her stern voice pulled me from my trance, and I found her standing up with her clothes already re-positioned.

"I'm sorry, but something that I forgot just slammed straight into my gut."

She nodded. "I can tell. You wanna talk about it?"

I quickly pulled my pants up my body. "No, it's kind of a private matter. I really have to go, but I want you to know that I enjoyed this. Whatever...*this* was."

She looked back at the bed. "Yeah, yeah. Me, too."

I raked my hand through my hair. "I'm sorry about this."

Her eyes came back to me. "No, no. Really, it's okay. Trust me, I get it. Sometimes I'll wake up at two in the morning with something I'd forgotten about that a dream reminded me of."

I smiled. "You do that, too?"

She giggled. "Yeah. I do that, too."

I cleared my throat and buried my smile. "Well, I'll see myself out. I hope you sleep well tonight, Ellie."

She winked. "Trust me, I will."

I chuckled as I leaned forward and placed a soft kiss against her cheek. "Goodnight."

She patted my chest. "Goodnight, Ryan."

And with every step I took away from her, I felt my heart calling out for me to go back. I felt my soul physically trying to turn me around as I stepped out the front door and closed it behind me. My mind knew that this was best, though. If I wanted a family, I needed to start prioritizing my family over whatever selfish whims I might have on a weekly basis.

Even if it meant letting go of a crush I had harbored for much, much too long.

Ellie

Bang! Bang! Ting!

I brought down the hammer against the cooling metal as I twisted and beat it into the shape I wanted it to take.

Bang! Bang! Ting!

I growled as I held tightly with the tongs seated against my gloves.

Bang! Bang! Ting!

"Why. Did he have. To leave?" I exclaimed, enunciating my words in time with my beating.

Bang! Bang! Ting!

Sweat poured down my face and my neck. I heard it sizzling as it hit the piping-hot metal instruments I was using to try to get a jumpstart on my latest project. I twisted the wrought iron into the shape I wanted it to be before hammering it into place once it cooled down a bit. Those little flattened elements really gave iron that modern sort of look everyone was going for nowadays. I figured I could carry around a small sample box of excess metal pieces showcasing my talents, which might help get clients while I was out and about doing regular, everyday things.

But, I was much too angry to focus.

"Shit," I hissed.

I'd been in my shop on my off-time for damn near three hours, and I had only accomplished blacksmithing six prime pieces that showed off my talents. And those six pieces didn't even cover a third of my range! I tossed the useless piece of wrought iron back into the tub before I slid it into the fire, watching as it bubbled and melted down into glowing, red-hot lava.

Then, I pulled it out with my gloved hands, poured it into the mold, and started from scratch.

"Come on, focus," I murmured to myself.

Perspiration saturated my body behind my work overalls, and my mask almost didn't stay on my head because of how wet my hair had become. Soot caked itself against my neck and the exposed places on my face, and I knew I'd need at least two scrub-downs to feel clean again after a day like this.

But, I had too much frustration and confusion to work out to be done with my day.

Thank fuck, the babysitter is staying later.

It took me a couple of days to register why I was so upset with Ryan. But, the more I worked with what was familiar to me, the more it came to me. I was pissed off that Ryan had left me so abruptly after something so intimate. It reminded me of my son's father; how he had tucked tail and ran for the hills the second we were done with our little moments of euphoria. For a split second at dinner, Ryan had made me feel like more than a hookup. Like more than a release. Like more than just some common means to an end.

Then, he did exactly what my ex had done.

"Fucking bullshit, if you ask me," I grunted.

Bang! Bang! Bang! Ting!

I mean, what the hell happened anyway? One minute, we were having a good time, and the next minute he was running away from me. For a moment there, I actually had contemplated asking him to spend the night. That was something I hadn't even shared with my son's father! We hadn't gotten to that point yet in our dating before I had gotten pregnant with Micah, and then it was like I had never existed.

Is that what's going to happen to Ryan?

"Well, not exactly like that," I said flatly.

It would have been easy to let him spend the night, too. I had it all thought out: he and I could curl up in bed and enjoy one another until the sun rose. Then, once Micah started whimpering and thrashing around in his bedroom, I could simply wake up Ryan and have him leave before I plucked Micah from his bed. Simple as that.

Bang! Bang! Bang! Bang! Tick!

"Goddammit, are you kidding?"

I watched as the piece of wrought iron I'd been working with for nearly a half an hour snapped in half. I mean, it was my fault, of course. But, still. Could nothing work in my favor this week? I ripped off my mask and picked up the pieces before tossing them back into the melting pot. But, when I looked at the handle to slide it back into the fiery kiln, I paused.

Did Ryan regret what happened between us?

"You're still working?" Sadie asked.

I jumped as I whipped around. "*Holy*... shit! You scared the hell out of me. Don't you people know I work with hot metal? Sneaking up on me isn't the safest thing for someone to do."

Sadie held up her hands in mock surrender. "I come in peace? You okay, Ellie?"

I sighed, wiping off my sweat with my forearm. "Yeah, just a long day."

She looked around my shop. "I can see that. Need help with anything?"

I snickered. "Nah, I've got it. Thanks, though."

"Uh-huh."

I turned my back to her. "So, what brings you into the shop? I don't think I've ever seen you down here before."

"Are you feeling okay?"

I snickered. "Yeah, never better. Why?"

"You want to turn around and try that lie again?"

I rolled my eyes. "Sadie, have you heard something that makes you feel as if something should be wrong with me?"

"I don't know. Is there something I should hear that I haven't?"

I slowly turned around. "I know this game you play, cousin. You think something's wrong, so you're alluding to the fact that you already know something to make me feel like I'm hiding something from you so I feel guilty enough to spill the beans."

Her eye twitched. "Is it working?"

I shook my head. "No."

She sighed. "Come on, Ellie. I know something's wrong. I can hear you banging against metal from clear across the field."

I blinked. "You can?"

She sighed. "Well, maybe not that much. But, you get my point."

I leaned against my workbench. "Yeah, yeah. I get your point."

She eyed me carefully. "Sure you don't want to talk about it?"

"Yeah, for now, at least, I'd like to just keep it to myself."

She walked up to me. "Then, would you like to bring Micah over for a little playdate tonight while Will and the guys are out?"

I peeked over at her. "The guys are going out tonight?"

She smiled triumphantly. "Courtesy of yours truly. I need a

damn break from that man, as much as I love him, and I could really use a glass of wine with my girls."

On the one hand, I wasn't sure if mixing alcohol with how I felt was a good idea. But, on the other hand, what the hell else did I have that was better to do? I scared men off so easily nowadays that it was almost comical to entertain the idea of inviting Ryan over for a do-over to try to get things right.

So, I smirked. "I'll bring a couple trays of snacks for us to munch on while we have wine."

Sadie giggled. "Fruit and veggies?"

"With the dip you like, girl. Always."

She threw her arms around me. "You're the best. You know that?"

I giggled. "You regretting that hug now?"

She slowly pulled away, shaking my sweat off her own skin. "Yeah, maybe just a tad."

I barked with laughter. "What time do you want us over?"

"Uh... you think you'll be okay to come over in an hour?"

I blinked. "What time is it?"

She pulled out her phone and showed me. "Almost six."

I unhooked my overalls. "Holy shit, I spent all damn day in here."

She swatted at my arm. "Don't worry, Mrs. Weatherford is keeping Micah at my place. The kiddos have been playing together all day. You just get home and get showered and come over whenever you're ready."

I started shutting down my equipment. "Sounds like a plan. See you soon!"

And as Sadie started out of my shop, I tried to get as pumped up for a girl's night as I could while praying Sadie didn't bring up this conversation we just had.

🦋 17 🦋

Ryan

"You're such an idiot," I hissed at the ceiling.

Two days later, I was still beating myself up over my abrupt leave from Ellie's place. On the one hand, I knew I was doing the right thing by not prolonging things like I wanted to. It wasn't fair to her, even if she didn't understand my personal life dynamics. I had decided to go through with the surrogacy and had even signed a contract with Leslie that outlined my financial responsibilities.

It was happening and bringing anyone into this kind of weird situation wasn't fair.

So, if I was doing the right thing, then why did I feel like such a jerk-off?

I slid my hands down my face and tried to talk myself out of how I felt. Over the past couple of days, I had worked damn near twenty-five hours just to keep my mind off things. And yet, something always came along at the most inopportune time to remind me of Ellie. Like the new hire at the headquarters and her eyes—they were the same color eyes as Ellie's, and every time we talked, I couldn't help but think of her.

Or my laundry. I had to wash my clothes from that night two times to get rid of Ellie's smell that lingered in my loft when I got back home from enjoying her.

If I concentrate, I can still smell her.

My eyes wanted to fall closed, so I'd concentrate harder, so I forced them to stay open. I wasn't sure what it was about this woman that had me completely addicted, but I had to cut it out. I was Ryan Remington, for crying out loud. I had control over myself. Over my emotions. Over my mental state. No woman did this to a man like myself. I was strong and capable and completely in control of my life.

Except for when she crosses my path and makes me weak in the knees.

"Dammit," I growled.

I forced myself to sit up in bed, and I picked up my phone. It was already five o'clock, and I still hadn't gotten through all of the shit I wanted to get done before the week really ramped up. I scratched the back of my head before reaching for a stack of folders sitting on the floor at my feet. I sat the stack of manila folders in my lap and started flipping through them, sorting the last of the resumes to hire for the last position available at HQ.

Then, once I found someone to take on the front-desk secretarial position, I could move on to other—more important—things, like fixing the hiccups we were already having with the refinery.

Before I could really get going on the folders, though, my phone started ringing. It wasn't a traditional phone call, though. Someone was attempting to FaceTime me. I reached mindlessly for my phone and picked up the call, figuring it was one of my brothers.

But, when I heard Leslie's voice, my folders went tumbling to the floor.

"Ryan? You okay?"

I leaped to my feet and tried to make myself look presentable. "Leslie! Hi! I didn't realize it was you calling."

She quirked an eyebrow. "You didn't look at the caller ID?"

I shrugged. "The only people who FaceTime me are my family."

Her jaw hit the floor. "I'm so sorry, this was very bold and brazen of me. I can call back tomorrow if—"

I shook my head. "No, no, no. Please, it's okay. Is something wrong?"

She held up some papers. "I just wanted to call you because I got your signed version of the contract, and there are a couple of things I want to ask you about."

I nodded. "Shoot."

She held the blurry paper up to the screen. "Can you see that?"

I chuckled. "Not really."

She sighed as she put it down. "Okay, well. That's line item four. It outlines any excess money you might feel the need to give me during our arranged surrogacy."

"Did I not allot you enough money? Because I have no problems changing that."

She snickered. "On the contrary, you allotted me about five times what the national average is. I wanted to check and make sure it wasn't a mistake or something."

I shrugged. "Why would it be?"

"Because if I don't use that money, I keep it. You know that, right?"

I nodded. "Yeah."

"And you really want to fork over an additional two hundred thousand dollars on top of what this is already costing you?"

I stared straight into her eyes. "Leslie, if things go according to plan, then you're about to do something my body can't do. You're about to give me the most precious gift on this planet that I have always wanted for myself. To me? Money isn't an object. I want you to be safe, taken care of, and I want you to have money to spend on yourself and splurge, or help you out with whatever might come after you give birth. Complications, or that PPD you were talking about. I want to make sure you're taken care of not just up to the birth, but through it and after it as well."

She snickered. "It's still incredibly generous."

"From what I've researched in the evenings, a woman's body goes through the most changes within the first two years, right? After they give birth?"

She nodded. "That's right."

"And I figured you and your husband's income combined is around the six-figure mark. Yes? Possibly a bit under?"

She paused. "A bit under, but yes. You'd also be right."

"Then, that's about two years' worth of your salaries that you can use for whatever you want, or need, after the birth. No questions asked. There's no reason for you guys to use your own money if you run into issues because of the pregnancy and birth that you then have to fork over your own personal money for. Doesn't make sense to me."

She sighed. "You're a good man, you know that?"

I don't feel like one right now. "I try my best."

Her eyes watered over. "Thank you, Ryan. Really."

"Is there anything else about the contract that's concerning to you?"

She sniffled as she wiped at her eyes. "Actually, that answers my other questions. Thank you for taking my call."

"Thank you for feeling comfortable enough to call."

"I'll get this signed and scanned back to you. Then from there, we can start looking at egg donation sites and figure out how you want to go about this."

I nodded. "Same time Sunday evening to discuss things?"

She smiled. "Same time, it is."

"Wonderful. You have a good night, Leslie."

"You too, Ryan."

After hanging up with my surrogate, I immediately dialed Valconie. Now that I had settled on someone, I was hoping he could refer me to a doctor in the area to help us. Or, possibly help me himself. I scrolled through my contacts and found his number before I pressed it as quickly as I could. And as I stood to my feet, I paced my small loft.

Trying to dispel as much nervous anxiety as I could before he picked up the phone.

"Ryan!"

I chuckled. "Hey, Val. How goes it?"

"Tell me you're calling with good news."

I grinned. "I'm calling with good news."

I heard him clapping in the background before his voice sounded again. "I take it the video interviews went well."

"I actually just finalized a contract with Leslie. She's signing it and sending it over to me tonight."

"Leslie. The blonde who's the stay at home mom?"

"That's the one."

I heard his smile through the phone. "She's great, isn't she? She plays the cello in her spare time, you know. She's a phenomenal player."

My eyebrows rose. "I didn't know that, actually. Do you know her personally or something?"

"Leslie and I actually dated for a spell way back in the day when we were younger."

My jaw dropped open. "You're fucking kidding me. And you let a good woman like her go?"

"Ah, it was one of my greatest regrets, until I met my wife. She'll do right by you, though. You made a good choice by picking her."

Relief settled in my stomach. "Well, that makes me feel better to hear."

He chuckled. "Have you had your lawyer look over the contract at all?"

"My lawyer was the one who drew up the contract, actually. We used the rudimentary one you sent over and expounded from there. I wanted it to be easy to understand but also cover all the necessary bases to protect all parties involved."

"Good, good. That'll serve you well in the long-run. And not going through a third-party agency with all of this is going to help maintain privacy, which I know you love."

I nodded. "Especially with something as sensitive as this. Val, I can't thank you enough for introducing us."

"Hey, you can thank me by naming your son Val."

I blinked. "Maybe a middle name. Or an honorable mention somewhere on the birth certificate."

He barked with laughter. "Don't worry, I hate my last name, too."

I grinned. "Any fun plans for your evening?"

"In the middle of the week? What kind of wild shit do you do with your family when you're out of town? I swear, you're all ties and suits and appointments in Dallas, but when you go home, you're day-drinking and shackin' up with women on a random Wednesday."

I chuckled. "Isn't it delightful?"

A knock came at my door, and Val laughed. "That sounds like your plan for the evening."

Will yelled from behind the door, "Open up, man!"

Wyatt hissed at him, "Can you not yell? Ryan hates that shit."

Bryce started pounding on the door. "Open up, Uncle Ryan! The boys are going out tonight."

I clicked my tongue. "Yep. You'd be right, Val."

He snickered. "Have fun and try not to die."

"I can promise the first but not the second."

He cackled with laughter. "I'm coming to visit you in Conroe sometime. You guys sound like a blast."

Boone rattled my doorknob. "Pull up your pants and stop stroking it! These beers won't drink themselves!"

I rolled my eyes. "They're going to kick my door down if I don't go."

"Then go, Ryan. Have fun. We can talk later."

I peeked over my shoulder at the folders strewn around my bed. "Yes, we'll talk later."

"All right, have fun. Bye."

"Bye."

I tossed my phone onto my bed and lunged for my door. And when I ripped it open, I saw Will hunched over, trying to pick my lock. I quirked an eyebrow as he slowly stood up with a sheepish look on his face, and my brothers couldn't stop trying to swallow back their laughter.

"Did you really think that would work?" I asked.

Will shrugged. "Worth a shot?"

I grinned. "A boys' night, huh? Where are the girls?"

Bryce patted Will's shoulder. "At Sadie and Will's place. The kids are running amok in the yard, and the girls are probably drinking wine."

I nodded slowly. "Well, that sounds safe."

Wyatt patted my shoulder. "They're good, you know they are."

Boone grinned. "And that means we get to go out and have some steaks."

Bryce nodded. "And beers."

I held my hands up in mock surrender. "Hey, you had me at steak, and I never need a reason to get a nice filet mignon. Let's go."

And as I reached for my jacket while thunder rumbled in the distance, I didn't get halfway out my damn door before my mind fell back to Ellie.

Ellie and those luscious lips of hers wrapped around the edge of a wine glass.

18

Ellie

"Cheers to girls' night!" Sadie exclaimed.

Willow, Luna, my cousin, and I clinked together our wine glasses full of a sangria that Luna threw together at the last minute. Wine sloshed over the edges, making us giggle as the kids ran around outside. I heard Sadie's animals neighing and baying and barking and clucking, and the entire time I couldn't wipe my smile off my face.

For once, I didn't have anything on my mind.

"Mm, this is so good," Willow said.

Sadie nodded as she wiped at her lips. "Ugh, I could chug this stuff."

Luna giggled. "Don't thank me. Ellie's the one who

brought the excess fruit. I just cracked open the wine and put it all in a nice jug."

I smiled. "And you're welcome. This fruit does pair really well with the red wine, though. We should definitely do this more often."

Sadie held up her glass. "Hear, hear!"

Us girls followed her spirit and mocked her motions. "Hear, hear!"

We all threw back our first glass of wine before Luna filled our cups up a second time. Then, we all walked out onto the back porch to watch the kids run around with the free-range animals. I giggled at how Anna-Marie tried to get onto the miniature donkey's back to ride around. Micah kept chasing the chickens and making "bawk" sounds that melted my heart. But, it was the screeching laughter of the twins as goats came up to lick their faces that made me giggle along with them.

"We've got some good kids, you know that?" Willow asked.

I sighed. "Really good kids, actually."

Thunder rumbled in the distance, and it froze the kids in the yard.

"You guys are okay!" Sadie exclaimed. "You can play until it starts to rain!"

Then, the kids all went back to doing what they were doing as if nothing happened.

"Your blackberry bushes have really grown up fast," Luna said.

Sadie giggled. "Come pluck yourself a basket, if you want. I'll never be able to use up all of these in one season, and that's with making jams, drinks, pies, cakes, cobblers, and canning some of them!"

My eyebrows rose. "That's a lot of things to do with blackberries."

"They're Will's favorite, so naturally, he planted way too many of them."

Willow smiled. "I bet the animals like them, though."

Sadie pointed. "That reminds me! I wanted to get y'all's opinion on free-range food."

I blinked. "Don't tell me you're about to kill those goats and eat them."

Sadie paused. "What? No! What in the world, Ellie?"

Luna and Willow fell apart in laughter as a smile crept across my cheeks. "I mean, when you say something like that with a yard full of animals, it's a logical conclusion."

Sadie shivered. "Yuck. No."

Luna sank down into her chair. "Plus, you never name anything you're going to eat. Helps with not getting emotionally attached."

Sadie's jaw dropped open. "You guys. I really can't think about eating my animals, okay?"

Willow rubbed her back. "It's all right. I'm sure the venison Bryce and Will keep exchanging with one another suits just fine, right?"

I pointed at her. "So long as you don't kill Bambi's mother. Don't do that shit."

Sadie's eyes widened. "All of you are horrible, you know that?"

I leaned forward in laughter before I cleared my throat. "Okay, okay, okay. What's this free-range food idea of yours?"

Sadie sighed. "Before we got horribly off-subject... Will and I were thinking about having two garden plots. One for us to live off of that's blocked off from our animals, and one that's specifically for our animals."

Luna paused. "Like, lettuce and spinach and tomatoes that they can just walk up and eat?"

Sadie nodded. "I thought it was a great idea, especially since we've had terrible issues with the chickens getting into our food here lately. If I can line the forest around the cabin or something like that with food that needs very little tending to during the spring and summer months, it'll help me with their feeding schedule and give them fresher foods to eat."

Willow crossed her legs. "I think it's a genius idea."

I sipped my wine. "Now that you've spelled it out, I'm wondering why other farmers don't do exactly this."

Sadie held out her hand. "Right? Now, just tell Will that so he'll stop bitching about it."

Luna waved her hand in the air. "Just do it anyway. What's he gonna do? He's at work all day!"

Sadie held out her arms, sloshing wine over the edge of her glass. "Right?"

The girls continued to talk about the "small garden" for her animals, and I gazed out toward the children. I watched Micah waddling around and playing tag, darting and weaving about through the shadows of the looming trees. I thought about the impact that not having a father around would eventually have on him, especially as a boy. I thought about the disservice I'd do to him, even if I tried to take up both roles. And the more I watched Micah, the more I wondered if Ryan had meant those things he had said about meeting Micah and cooking us breakfast and getting to know my son.

Did he ever mean them?

"Yoo-hoo! Earth to Ellie!" Sadie called out.

I came to with someone waving their hand in front of my face, and it made me jump. "What the fuck?"

Willow giggled. "You good over there?"

Luna freshened up my wine. "Got something on your mind you want to talk about?"

I puffed out my cheeks with a sigh. "Nah, not really. Just a long day."

Sadie smirked. "A long day slamming a hammer against iron after work hours, am I right?"

The girls all looked at me before Willow cleared her throat. "It's been a while since you've worked after hours like that. You sure you're okay?"

I set my wine onto the table in front of me. "It's really nothing."

Luna leaned toward me. "Does 'nothing' have a name that rhymes with 'Brian'?"

I rolled my eyes. "I really hate y'all sometimes, you know that?"

Willow clapped her hands together. "I knew it! I knew he was on your mind. I've been watching you, you know."

I murmured to myself, "Awkward."

Willow brushed off my comment. "And I see how you have eyes for Ryan. How you watch him whenever he's around. How you stare at him while he's talking with you."

I blinked. "Should I... should I *not* stare at the man while he's talking with me?"

She shoved my shoulder playfully. "You know damn good and well what I mean."

I felt my cheeks blushing. "Look, it's really nothing."

Sadie pointed at me. "Says the girl who's blushing."

I shot her a look, and Sadie quickly rolled her lips over her teeth, but the girls saw it, too.

"What was that all about?" Willow asked.

Luna kicked her feet up onto the table. "Now, I'm jealous. There's a story here we don't know, isn't there?"

Sadie sighed. "Guys, why don't we just leave this be for a little bit. I think it's making Ellie uncom—"

Willow held up her hand, cutting off my cousin. "Oh, no, no, no. You don't get to tease us with cheeky little Ellie, then shut up Sadie with a look, and us just go on about our night like it didn't happen. Spill the beans, gorgeous."

Sadie's face hardened. "Willow, for real. You've got no idea what she's been through."

I sighed. "It's okay, really. I think it's about time I started talking about it, anyway."

Sadie's eyes grew worrisome. "Are you sure?"

Luna cleared her throat. "Talk about what?"

Silence fell over the table as I took a long pull from my wine. "I mean, talking about what really happened between Micah's father and myself."

I knew it wasn't fair to keep the girls in the dark, especially with how much they had helped my son and me. They had earned the right to know what had brought me to Conroe during the last stages of my pregnancy. They had earned the right to know why the men they loved were helping me as much as they were. And it made it even worse now that they knew Sadie knew.

It seemed sorely unfair, and I didn't want to destroy the relationships I had worked so hard to build in this area.

"Whenever you're ready, I've got your back," Sadie said.

So, I drew in a deep breath. "I always knew college wasn't for me. I lived in this smaller town on the outskirts of Dallas, and I never saw myself going into the big city and taking more pointless tests and more meaningless classes when I didn't want a traditional life in the first place. So, when I graduated, I packed up my things and found a job as a farmhand on one of the larger ranches there in Dallas. And that's where I met my ex."

The girls nodded and listened as I drew in another deep breath.

"We clicked right from the very beginning, and he's the one who introduced me to blacksmithing. He took me under his wing and taught me the basics until I saved up enough money as a ranch hand to afford an eight-week crash course in farrier training. Then, I had to do a four-year apprenticeship underneath someone already registered as a farrier. So, it only made sense to do the apprenticeship with Michael."

"Your ex," Willow said.

I nodded. "Yeah. We weren't dating at that time. Honestly, I don't think we were dating at all—ever. I mean, we'd go out to dinner and split the bill. Sometimes, we'd go out dancing before we'd hook up or whatever, but it was more of a relationship in my mind than a spoken agreement. And it went on like that through the majority of my four-year apprenticeship. Then, I got pregnant with Micah."

Luna gasped. "No, he didn't."

I nodded. "Yes, he did. I fell in love with a man who I thought wanted me, and the second I told him I was pregnant, he turned his back. He blocked my number. He passed off the last two months of my apprenticeship to another guy in town. Michael even got himself transferred off the ranch we were living and working on together." It wasn't a pretty picture then, and it didn't sound any better now.

Willow's jaw dropped open. "That sorry excuse for a shitbag."

My eyes lined with tears. "It was single-handedly the hardest thing to accept. Thankfully, the man who finished my last two months of my apprenticeship didn't ask many questions. And I honestly learned more in those two months than I had at any point in time beneath Michael."

"Do you know where he is at all? Has he ever popped back up?" Luna asked.

I shook my head slowly. "Not a damn clue. I don't know where he went or what he's doing, and I honestly don't care. He's a sack of shit, and I hope he gets hit by a bus." I shouldn't feel that way about anyone, but I did; pretending any differently would be a lie.

Willow took my hand. "That's the spirit."

I scoffed, "That's why, even though I know I have a crush on Ryan, I shouldn't be getting into anything right now. I'm still healing from so much and not just things that I went through with Micah's father."

"You know Ryan's a good man, right?" Luna asked.

Yeah, that's why this sucks. "I know he is."

"And you know he'd accept Micah as his own, right?" Willow asked.

Sadie interjected, and I was glad for it. "Things are just still raw for her, that's all. I agree with her decision not to make something of it, too. There's no need to rush into anything she's not ready for."

"You should at least talk to Ryan. Tell him how you feel but why you can't—or won't—act on it. I mean, I see the way he looks at you when you aren't looking. He's got the same crush," Willow said.

I blinked. "Really? He does?"

The truth of the matter was that I wanted to talk to Ryan. I really did. I wanted him to know how I felt. But, I knew what our talking would lead to. And I knew what he wanted out of his life, which was something I wasn't situated to give him. Now or ever—I couldn't.

I squeezed Willow's hand. "I appreciate the support and you guys listening to me, but for now, I just need to focus on myself and this business. Things are going really well, and I don't want to ruin that momentum because I can't keep my eye on the prize. That's all."

Luna patted my shoulder. "Then, we support you one hundred percent."

I smiled softly. "Thanks, girls. I really appreciate it."

Willow released my hand. "Anytime, girl. Anytime."

What's the hurt in having a little fun?

As the girls started talking again, my mind began betraying me. It did this all the time, and I was sick of it. This was exactly the kind of shit my mind told me before I fell in love with my ex. My mind kept talking me into "having a little fun" and "letting loose" and "being a modern woman." And then I tripped and fell into a slew of emotions I had no business feeling for a man who blatantly showed me I was nothing more than a hook-up.

It's not like you can have another baby-daddy scenario.

The thought drained me of any happiness I had still seated inside of me. I threw the rest of my wine back before standing to my feet and excusing myself to the bathroom. I quickly made my way inside and opened every door until I found it. Then, I locked myself inside and splashed some cool water onto my face.

Anything to mask the tears sliding down my cheeks. "Dammit," I whispered.

I had left Dallas and flew here to get closer to the only

shred of a family I had remaining and to ditch my sadness in the past. I had left Dallas to get away from the bad memories and even worse decisions. I had come to Conroe to start again. To plant Micah in a place that would love him, no matter who his parents were.

So, how the fuck did my sadness follow me all the way here?

Because you can't move forward.

I yanked a towel off the hanger next to me and dabbed at my face. Tears still streaked my skin, finding their death against my jawline as I stared at my empty eyes in the mirror. Was this what I had been reduced to? Was this what I had allowed Michael to do to me after all this time? Just chisel away at my happiness until there was nothing left?

"He can't have that kind of control," I hissed.

So, I hung the towel back up and dried my tears for good. At least, I hoped they were dried up for good. Because I was getting damn tired of spending my free hours at night crying myself to sleep.

19

Ryan

Bryce high-fived Will over my head while Wyatt drove us to the steakhouse across town. I knew Bart and Boone were meeting us there, which meant a full house of brotherly love and throwing back shots. But, as we rode in Bryce's massive truck toward the restaurant, I couldn't help but think of Ellie and the girls and what they were getting up to.

"So! How are the new hires coming along?" Wyatt asked.

Before I could even answer his question, the guys started booing him.

"No work talk!" Bryce exclaimed.

Will cackled with laughter. "Work is boring! Drinks are better! Work is boring! Drinks are better!"

Wyatt grumbled, "What are we, frat boys?"

Bryce and Will high-fived again. "Yay, for frat boys!"

I rolled my eyes as Bryce soared down the highway, and it almost felt like I was back in college. This was the kind of shit I got up to with my friends while trying to get my business degree, and I wasn't into it anymore. Nevertheless, I hadn't had a decent steak since my lunch with Val, so I was ready to sink my teeth into a bacon-wrapped filet mignon coated in a rich mushroom sauce.

The only thing that would have made it better, though, was Ellie.

As I gazed out the window and watched the countryside pass by, a nagging feeling scratched at the inside of my skull. Something didn't sit right with me, especially after my last encounter with Ellie, and I wanted a chance to speak with her about it. I didn't want there to be tension between the two of us. I didn't want her thinking that she had done something wrong or screwed something up.

You know that's not the issue.

I pushed the little voice in my head off to the side because it did me no good to evaluate what it meant. I knew there was something Ellie kept hidden away from the world. Something that was affecting her big time. And I didn't hold a place in her life to be clawing at something like that, although I wished I did. Did I want to know? Of course. I was curious about it and curious about her, and I wanted to know everything she was open to telling me. But, if there were something that sensitive that she kept close to her heart, I had no place in her life to go poking around for it.

I wanted to have a place like that, though.

"The fuck's on your mind tonight?" Bryce asked.

Will nudged me. "If I didn't know any better, I'd say you were thinking about Ellie."

Wyatt snickered. "Even I see how he stares off after her."

Bryce lowered his voice. "Did he ever tell anyone what he and Ellie did after that barn party?"

Wyatt shook his head. "Didn't even tell Boone and me."

I cleared my throat. "I can hear you assholes."

Will chuckled. "Good! Because we're all about to explode. Spill the details, man. What the hell did you and Ellie do after that dance?"

I shrugged. "We had a bit too much to drink, and I didn't want Ellie walking home alone like that."

Wyatt scoffed. "And now that you have the lie out of the way, you can tell us the truth."

I shook my head and let it roll off my back because I sure as hell wasn't telling them what was going on. I needed to figure this out on my own like a man, and I definitely didn't need my brothers hounding me or teasing me about it. No, I didn't date much. Yes, whenever I hooked up with someone it was big news. But, who the fuck cared?

My life, my rules.

"Maybe if I tell you that we know you've been drinking alone again, you'll lean on us for support, then," Wyatt said.

The truck fell silent as we pulled into the parking lot of

the steakhouse. The smells alone dragged me out of the truck without answering the question, but I felt their prying eyes on my back. What I did to mend a broken heart was my business and my business alone. I still needed to talk to Ellie, though.

"Hey, you guys?" I asked. I turned around and found all of them staring at me before Bryce spoke.

"Let me guess—you're about to get a cab home because something just came up."

I blinked. "No. I need to get a cab home because I need to speak with Ellie about something."

Will patted my shoulder. "My man! You go get your woman."

I shook my head. "Not like that."

Bryce cocked his head. "Everything okay?"

My cheeks puffed out with a sigh. "Will you just tell Bart and Boone I said hey? I really gotta go."

Wyatt nodded. "Yeah, yeah, sure. And I'll make sure to get you dinner to-go."

I nodded. "I appreciate that. Really."

After clapping their backs and sending them into the restaurant, I walked toward the main road. There weren't many taxis in the small town of Conroe, but there were a few Uber drivers here and there. I opened up the app on my phone and hailed for a ride, and ten minutes later, I found myself slipping into the back of an old pick-up truck. An elderly man gave me a very smooth, quiet ride back to the ranch, so I tipped him well before I started on my journey, hiking across the property until I stood face to face with the guesthouse front door.

"Here goes nothing," I murmured to myself.

I knocked on the door and waited for Ellie to open up, but I didn't hear any sounds behind the door. I furrowed my brow and knocked again before checking my watch, and sure enough, it was almost seven-thirty. I figured Ellie would've been back from hanging out with the girls and knee-deep in spending time with her son or something.

But, there wasn't even a light turned on inside.

"Ellie?" I asked to no one.

I scooted over to the front windows and tried peeking through. But, the blinds were drawn and I couldn't see inside. I marched around to the side of the guesthouse and cupped my hands against the glass, peering in to make sure everything was okay. And just as I was about to make my way around to the back of the house, a voice emanated from behind me.

The sweetest, most angelic sound to ever grace my ears said, "I didn't realize we had a peeping Tom," Ellie said.

I turned to face her and saw how red her cheeks were. The sweat dripped down from her brow as she cradled her sleeping son in her arms, and I immediately rushed to her. Without another word spoken, I scooped Micah into my arms so she could dig out her keys. And as I watched her walk into the place she called home, I paused on the welcome mat.

Was I allowed inside?

"You coming or what?" she called out.

I stepped over the threshold. "What can I help you with?"

She pointed. "Door on the right is his room. Can you go lay him down?"

I walked past her as she put on a pot of coffee. "What, then?"

She sighed. "Uh... pajamas are the top drawer of his dresser. Pick out a pair, and I'll come change him in a second."

"You sure you don't want me to do that?"

She peeked around the corner of the kitchen. "Do you know *how* to do that?"

I shrugged. "Isn't dressing a kid kind of like dressing myself?"

She snickered and waved me off. "If you think it is, then be my guest."

I wasn't sure what she meant by that, but anything I could do to help her, I'd do. So, I slipped into Micah's bedroom and turned on his bedside lamp. I laid him down on his tiny mattress that looked like it belonged in a miniature house instead of a full-sized bedroom. I couldn't help but smile as I picked through his pajamas. His tiny little pants with cuffs around the ankles boasting of cars and sports and rainbows made me smile.

"Here we go, this one should do," I whispered.

I walked back over to Micah and started with his feet. Off came his shoes and his incredibly stinky socks before I tried to wiggle him out of his little jeans. But, every time I tried moving him, he'd shift and almost wake up. I had to tug and wait. Tug and wait. Tug and wait some more.

However, I finally understood what Ellie meant when I started putting on his pajama pants.

Everything those damned things could snag on, they did. Everything they could catch on, they did—a toe, a knee, a baby butt. And every time I shifted Micah too much, he'd almost wake up. It took me damn near twenty minutes just to get him changed, and then there was wiping him down a bit since he smelled sweaty. I didn't like going to bed dirty, so I figured a little boy probably didn't, either.

I wiped against his brow and under the fold of his neck. I picked up his arms gingerly and cleaned his pits down before easing a shirt over his tired little head. He rolled away from me and started reaching around for something, so I quickly handed him a little stuffed animal that was tossed into a corner.

Then, I pulled a small blanket over his tiny little body and watched him fall right back asleep.

"You're a natural," Ellie said from the doorway.

I whipped around and had to hold back a curse. "Jesu —holy—"

She giggled. "Did I scare you?"

I slid my hand through my hair. "A bit?"

She giggled and nodded down the hallway. "Come on. I made coffee."

I walked out of Micah's room and closed the door softly behind me. And as I sat down at the small kitchen table, I made myself a strong and sugary mug of coffee. It woke me up enough to see the distress lines in Ellie's forehead. It woke me up enough to see the worry dancing behind her gorgeous eyes. She looked as if she had words on the tip of her tongue that she simply couldn't spit out, and I wondered if it was because I was here.

Just grow a sack and ask her, idiot.

And apparently, her brain was doing the same thing. Because when we spoke, we spoke in unison.

"I can't get you off my mind," I said quickly.

"What are we doing?" she asked.

I furrowed my brow. "That's actually a better topic of conversation than what I had in mind."

She blinked. "You can't get your mind off me?"

I snickered. "No, I can't."

She smiled softly. "Me, neither. I mean, for you, that is."

The tension came rushing back, and I drew in a deep breath. I knew Ellie was hiding something. It was etched all over her face. But, did I have a right to bring it up? Did I have a right to force it out of her? It wasn't as if we were together or anything? We weren't dating or seeing each other formally. Hell, this was the first time we'd had a decent conversation that most certainly wouldn't lead to sex. So, what right did I have to ask her about something like this?

Why the hell is this shit so hard? "How is your new job coming along? You know, with your repeat customers?"

She sighed. "They're coming along all right. What I'm doing right now is trying to get a jumpstart on shoes for the horses and stuff so I don't fall behind in my work for the rodeos."

"I'm sure you're doing just fine in both arenas. And you know Bryce will always want you to focus on your business before the horses."

She shook her head. "He and I have an agreement, and I will uphold it to its fullest extent. I don't want there to be any contention when it comes time for me to pull away, if that makes any sense."

I nodded. "Makes perfect sense."

The two of us sipped our coffee simultaneously, and it made both of us giggle. But, all too soon, that tension came rushing back again. And not the good kind, either.

How did I even start a conversation like this?

Just run, Ryan. It's not like she'll ever accept your life.

I knew Ellie was better than that, though.

She'll want your money, in the end. Just like every other girl.

I definitely knew Ellie was better than that, too. She was more independent than any woman I'd ever come across back in Dallas. And she constantly left me in awe of what she could accomplish.

If she can't talk to you now, she won't talk to you then.

An easy thing to remedy if I simply took the reins and stopped being a little chicken-shit.

You're about to have a kid with a surrogate. You really think she's gonna just be okay with that?

She was a single mother, and I was completely okay with her having a child. Why was my situation any different?

"Why did I find you peeking through my windows?" Ellie finally asked.

Her voice pulled me from the recesses of my mind, and I figured it was now or never. I'd never get another perfect chance like this one to speak with Ellie, one on one. She kept herself busy, and I had a feeling it had something to do with what filled up the space behind her eyes. And while I worried my line of questioning and pushing might really end something between us before we could get it off the ground, the little voice in my head did have a point.

If she couldn't talk to me now, what made me think she'd be able to talk with me down the line? My mother raised me with the one truth about dating that had always stuck with me, through my childhood as well as my adult years. She'd said, "Dating is as good as it gets, Ryan. Things don't magically appear after someone gets married. Remember that."

So, what better way to tackle a possible communication issue than to simply blow the doors right off the damn thing?

❦ 20 ❦

Ellie

Ryan looked so lost, yet so determined. Almost as if he were having an argument with himself. And while part of that made me nervous, the other part of me was ready. I might never know what could have been between myself and Ryan, but at least if I were honest with him, I wouldn't have any regrets about the situation.

But when he started talking, it only made me feel worse.

"I have feelings for you, Ellie."

I blinked. "You do?"

He scooted to the edge of his chair and took my hand in his. "Yes, I really do. You're fucking magnetic, you know that? You've been in Conroe for a little over two years or so now—"

I nodded. "Almost three."

He grinned. "Yes, almost three. And during the entire time you've been around, I haven't once been swayed or tempted or even had an inkling to date."

I furrowed my brow. "You haven't?"

He shook his head. "Not one bit. I figured it was just me growing up, growing out of my boyish ways, or possibly getting too busy with work. But, it was you, Ellie. From the first time I ever laid eyes on you and shook your hand—or had an ounce of conversation with you—I knew there was no other woman who would ever amount to who you are. You'd pale them. Overshadow them. And I knew if I went on any dates, I'd only be asking myself why I didn't have the balls to ask you."

I blinked back tears before they formed. "You—really, Ryan?"

He squeezed my hand. "Yes, really. It's a pleasure anytime I run into you, and the little bit of time we've spent together these past couple of weeks have had me on cloud nine. There's something about you that I can't shake, and I'd like to take the time to explore whatever it is that I feel for you. If you'd like that, that is."

I didn't know what to say. For a minute there, I lost the capability to speak. Had I heard Ryan correctly? Was he really pouring out his heart and soul to a girl like me? I fully expected to wake up from some sort of dream and be slouched over in my recliner with Micah in my lap. I fully expected to jolt awake in the middle of the night, sweating profusely in my bed with heat between my thighs. But, the more I blinked and the more I tried to clear out the dream, the stronger my reality became.

What the hell did a handsome, level-headed, rich-ass, salt-and-pepper-haired slice of perfection want with a single mother like me?

"You can't be serious," I finally said.

Ryan blinked—twice. "Uh, well, I am."

I pulled my hand away from his. "That is a lot, Ryan."

His shoulders slumped a bit. "I know. I know I'm being a bit hasty. But, I guess all of this is just mounting up to asking you out to dinner. Formally, you know? And not dinner that's masked as a celebration and not dinner that's masked as a party. But, an actual date."

I blinked. "Wait a second, our barbecue outing was a date?"

He paused. "I treated it as such. But, I wasn't under the impression that you were."

I fell back against my chair. "Holy shit."

He pulled his chair around the table to get closer. "I'd apologize for coming on too strong, but I'm not sorry. You deserve a man who will tell you what's on his mind, even if it scares the shit out of him."

"I don't even wear dresses!" I blurted out.

He paused. "Um, what?"

I threw my hands into the air. "Willow, and Sadie, and Luna. They're all so cute and country...and girls!"

He nodded slowly. "Yes, yes, they are. Good observation."

I stood to my feet. "And me? The only dress I own, I

burned after the barn dance because it was a dress my ex gave me!"

"Wait, you burned that dress? I thought it looked great on you."

"Not the point!" I squeaked.

"Right, right. Not the point."

I pinched the bridge of my nose. "I'm a tomboy, at best, Ryan. I don't do heels, and jewelry, and makeup, and fashion. I don't own dresses, and I don't go to fancy restaurants, and even if I wanted to do all of that stuff, I'm just not coordinated enough. You want to know why all of my shirts match my pants? Because I wear jeans all the time, that's why. You want to know why all of my socks match? They don't! Because I don't give a shit about matching socks! And you can forget home-cooked meals. I mean, I do okay in the kitchen, but it's nothing spectacular. I'm certainly not cut out to be a stay-at-home mother, either. I tried to rely on a man once, and he fucking up and left me in the dust. And I don't want that to happen again. I'm better than that, you know?"

By the time I was done with my tirade, I felt myself panting. My knees felt weak, and I found myself staring at Ryan's chest.

When did he stand up?

"Ellie, look at me."

I swallowed hard. "I am."

He chuckled as he crooked his finger beneath my chin, pulling my gaze to his. "There you are."

"Ah, like this."

He cupped my cheek. "Like this."

I nuzzled against his palm. "We're two peas in separate pods, you know."

"That's what you think, sure. Because you see the kinds of women you're surrounded by, and you think that's what I want."

My eyes danced between his. "Isn't that what you want?"

He shook his head. "I'm looking at what I want."

His lips dropped to mine, and the bones in my body evaporated. His arms cloaked my back as he held me against him, and I clung to him with all my might. Tears rushed the backs of my eyes as he sat back down into his chair, carrying me with him until I seated myself into his lap. Our tongues fell together effortlessly, and for a moment, I was the princess in the castle who had found her knight in shining armor.

But, when he pulled his lips away, the fantasy was over. And I was back to being the damaged single mother trapped in an endless cycle of perpetual bullshit.

"Ryan, I can't," I whispered.

He tucked my hair behind my ear. "I understand that's how you feel because of insecurities from your past, but I promise you it isn't the truth."

I slid off his lap and plopped back into my chair. "No, it's not that."

"It's not what?"

"It's not my insecurities, though I do have some."

He chuckled. "I'm becoming aware of that."

I glared at him. "That's not what I'm talking about. I actually cannot be with you. Ever."

He blinked. "Now, you have me curious. What has you so convinced?"

I shrugged. "I know what you want out of life, and I can't give that to you."

"Money?"

"What?"

"Because if you're talking about money, I already have loads of it."

I snickered. "Yeah, no. Not money."

"A job? Because I have that, too."

I rolled my eyes. "Not funny, Ryan."

"Is it a car? I don't need a car. Though, people in Dallas think I need a car."

"I don't mean—wait. They don't like your truck? I love your truck."

He snapped his fingers and pointed at me. "Which is why you're perfect for me."

I shook my head. "No, I'm not."

He waved his hand at me. "I don't care about homecooked meals, anyway. I throw down a mean pasta dish in the kitchen, and as long as you can whip up a salad, we've got a full meal right there. Maybe one day, Micah can throw some garlic bread into the oven, and we've got ourselves the perfect Friday family dinner right there."

I wanted to tell him. I needed to tell him. Everything inside of me screamed to tell him. But, I liked what Ryan was talking about too much. Even if it was nothing but a distant fantasy or dream, I enjoyed living in it. Even if I knew it couldn't come to fruition.

So, I tabled my concerns and smiled. "That actually sounds nice."

He leaned forward and reached his hands out for me. "See? This can work if you just toss out your preconceived notions of the kind of life you think I should have. Okay?"

I slid my hands into his. "Okay, I can do that."

He smiled. "Great. So, without further waiting. Ellie?"

"Yes?"

"Would you—and Micah, if you want to bring him along— like to have dinner with me sometime?"

I smiled. "I don't think it'll take much to get Mrs. Weatherford to stay a bit longer with him for a day."

"Actually, I was thinking more of an overnight sort of thing."

I paused. "Oh?"

He nodded. "Maybe even two nights?"

I felt a bit deflated. "Oh."

"And even if it's just one night, that's completely okay. But, I thought about maybe getting us a room somewhere after dinner. You know, just in case. That way, if things go further, we have a space that's all ours. You won't be worried about Micah because it'll all be planned for in advance. And I'm sure it's been a while since you've gotten away on your own for a night."

I blinked. "Actually, yeah. It has been a while. Since well before my son was born."

"See? All the more reason to do this. I was originally planning for an entire weekend, but I don't have any issues with just a Friday—or even Saturday—night. Whatever works the best for you."

I tossed the idea around in my mind. "Is it possible to plan for a weekend, but get a place that might refund you for a night in case there's an emergency with Micah?"

"I'll do you one better. If after our first night you wake up and you're missing him that much, we can go get him, and he can spend the other night in the hotel with us."

My jaw dropped open in shock. "You'd really do that?"

He smiled softly. "Micah is part of you, and it's a part of you I'd love to get to know better. I know you're a packaged deal, for lack of a better phrase, and I'm all for it. I won't leave him out. I will always make contingencies for him, whatever makes you feel more comfortable."

I sighed. "How are you so perfect?"

He chuckled. "Not perfect, but possibly perfect for you?"

I leaned forward and captured his lips softly, sealing our pending date with a kiss. He released my hands and cupped my cheeks, pressing harder against my mouth. I moaned as we wiggled away from the table. We enveloped one another as I lost myself in his muscles. In his heat. In the taste of his tongue and the way his cock stiffened against my body. Ryan touched a part of me that hadn't been touched in so long. He made me feel beautiful and wanted and worth something.

And I couldn't wait to get Sadie on the phone to tell her.

"Mmm, definitely more of that in the future," he hummed against my lips.

I giggled. "Yes. Definitely."

He sighed. "Well, I better leave and let you get some sleep before I keep you up all night."

"I'd try to fight with you on that if I didn't have an early day tomorrow."

He kissed my forehead softly. "Me, too. No worries there."

I closed my eyes. "Let me know when you have the final plans for things, and I'll talk to the nanny, okay?"

He led me toward the front door. "I can definitely do that. How does next weekend sound?"

I pecked the swell of his exposed bicep. "Sounds perfect."

He scooped me into one last heated kiss before I got him out the front door, and the second it closed, I rushed to get to my cell phone. I needed to call Sadie. I needed to fill her in on what had just happened so I could calm myself down. I felt like a giddy high school girl who had just been asked to the senior prom by the quarterback of the fucking football team.

And I knew I wouldn't get a lick of sleep tonight if I didn't talk about this before trying to go to bed.

21

Ryan

I straightened the tie on my suit before knocking on the guesthouse door. I slid my hands into my pockets, hoping and praying that tonight went off without a hitch. I'd gone through a hell of a lot of trouble securing what I needed to in a short period, and all I wanted was for Ellie to enjoy herself to the fullest.

But, I wasn't nearly prepared for her when she opened the door.

"Hey there, handsome," she said with a smile.

I parted my lips in an attempt to speak, but I simply couldn't. Ellie had taken her version of "dressed to the nines" and put a fresh new spin on it that had my jaw swinging against the concrete porch. Her blond hair was down in beautiful waves, falling past her shoulders and acting as an angelic halo around her perfect little head. She had on a pair of heels that were just high enough to flex those smooth, luscious legs of hers, and the dress she donned was navy blue, and it fell just off her shoulders. The dress's waist cinched in just enough to take in her curves while leaving a taste of the unknown beyond the fabric, and the smallest bit of makeup she had on accented the deep-blue color of her eyes and the soft, natural-pink pout of her pillowy lips.

"My God," I whispered.

She giggled. "Too much?"

I shook my head slowly. "Ellie, you look..." My eyes slid up her body before our eyes met. "You look breathtaking."

Her cheeks blushed, and I had just enough mental forethought to offer her my arm. She had me stunned into silence, and I couldn't wait to show her the weekend I had planned for us. I was the luckiest man in the world to have a woman like her by my side for the next couple of days, and as she slid her arm into mine, I felt a heat trickle all the way down to my toes.

I love this woman, and I'm not even afraid to admit it.

The thought dawned on me so naturally and so fluidly that my heart took flight. I never felt quite at home until Ellie was on my arm. I never felt quite alive enough until Ellie's voice filled my ears. And whenever I had her naked body pressed against me, the rest of the world didn't matter. I had fallen head over heels for this gorgeous beach babe that had been dropped into the middle of a country setting, and her tomboyish nature only served to make me feel right where I was supposed to be.

"So," Ellie said as I helped her into my truck, "where are we headed for dinner?"

I grinned. "It's a surprise and one I hope you enjoy."

Her hand held mine the entire way to the restaurant. And while we didn't say anything to one another, it was a comfortable silence. With other women, I felt the need to fill the space, to mindlessly talk and make myself appear more engaging than normal. But, with Ellie? The silence between us was comfortable. We were with one another, but we weren't overwhelmed by one another, and I adored that about us.

However, once I pulled into the Italian restaurant, Ellie gasped.

"You didn't," she said.

I parked the truck and looked over at her. "I didn't what?"

Her eyes slowly panned toward mine. "How in the world did you get us reservations at this place?"

I chuckled. "You know about this place?"

"Everyone knows about this place!"

I unbuckled my seatbelt. "Well, come with me and let's get a firsthand account. Yeah?"

The fact that I had already impressed her made my chest puff with pride. But, the night was young, and my surprises were only beginning. I ushered her into the restaurant on my arm, and the entire room turned to look at her. The second she walked in, I saw men trying not to stare and women smacking the back of their husband's heads while they blatantly gazed at the beautiful, leggy blonde on my arm for the evening.

And if I played my cards right this weekend, she'd be on my arm for good.

"Name?" the host asked.

"Reservation for two, Ryan Remington," I said.

Ellie giggled as the man peeked down at his reservation book. "Ah, a last-minute reservation. You must have some pull here, Mr. Remington. Right this way, not a moment to lose! Your menu has already been curated and prepared."

"Our menu?" Ellie asked.

I smiled down at her. "Just go with the flow. Enjoy it, okay?"

The host walked us through a couple of rooms full of booths and tables before bringing us to a door. And when he threw open the door, the comforting heat of the crackling fire drew us both inside. Ellie gasped as she released my arm, walking over toward the table in the middle of the room. The silky black tablecloth across the rounded table set for two was topped with a rose, a flickering candle, and two glasses of red wine already prepared for us.

I slipped the host a tip for his troubles on the last-minute additions before he left us.

"This is all for us?" Ellie asked as she turned around.

I walked over to her seat and pulled it out. "Care to sit? Our appetizers should be out any—"

Our waitress slinked quietly into the room. "Did someone say appetizers?"

I held my hand out for her. "See? Told you."

Ellie shook her head as she sat in her seat, then I scooted her softly underneath the table. I made quick work of sitting in across from her just as the waitress set our oysters on ice in front of us, and Ellie wrinkled her nose.

"What in the world?" she asked.

I chuckled. "Never had an oyster?"

She looked at me, hesitantly. "Only when they've been deep-fried."

I scooped one up. "You might be thinking of clams. Here, I'll show you how to eat them. They're really good if you know the technique."

She blinked. "There's a technique?"

I snickered. "Just bring that beautiful ass over here and sit on my knee, would you?"

With a smile and a giddy laugh, she got up and came over to me. Ellie sat on my thigh before I ran my spoon around the bottom of the oyster, dislodging it from its shell. Then, I sprinkled a bit of melted butter on top, added some pepper, and then I held it up to her lips.

"Now, the key is to swallow it down. Don't chew it too much, okay?" I asked.

She peeked down at me. "Food I'm not supposed to chew? That doesn't sound natural."

I chuckled. "Just try it. If you don't like it, then you don't have to eat anymore. Okay?"

She sighed. "All right, you asked for it."

I held it up to her lips, and she slurped it into her mouth.

And when a small trail of juice trickled down her chin, I wiped it away with my thumb. She swallowed almost instantly, and I watched her face for even the smallest reaction.

Then, she pointed to the red sauce on the table. "Could I try another one with that?"

I grinned. "Of course, you can. You can try anything you want."

We went back and forth, feeding one another oysters, and I'd never felt closer to someone in all my life. We talked and giggled between bites, and the more the conversation flowed between us, the more I wondered why the hell I had tiptoed around her for so fucking long.

Ellie stood from my lap. "Wow, those were actually pretty good. I get why you shouldn't chew them, though. They're practically rubber if you do."

I snickered. "Yeah, they aren't meant to be enjoyed with your teeth."

She smirked. "I also now understand why they're an aphrodisiac."

I almost choked on my wine. "Sorry, what?"

She barked with laughter. "Nothing! You didn't hear it from me."

But, I did hear it. I had heard every syllable of it. And my mind spun with all of the things we could do once we got back to the hotel suite I had rented for the weekend. And Micah, if she wanted to pick him up tomorrow.

However, I'd set into motion some plans for Micah that, hopefully, granted me a full weekend with her at my side.

"I'm so sorry, my phone is buzzing with text messages, and I think it's the girls. Do you mind if—?"

I waved my hand at her. "Check anything you want. I'm hoping for a very specific text message to roll through from Sadie anyway."

She eyed me quizzically. "Really now?"

I grinned. "I think you'll like it, so don't worry about it."

She pulled out her phone and rifled through the messages, but when she didn't smile, I figured my last part of the plan hadn't happened yet. She turned off her phone and slid it back into a pocket in her dress that I didn't even know she had on her dress.

When her eyes met mine, though, I knew something was wrong.

"What is it? Is it Micah?" I asked.

She sighed. "Sadie told me a few minutes ago that she and Will just picked him up, and he's ready to spend the night."

I breathed a sigh of relief. "Oh, good. They got him, then."

She paused. "Is that your surprise?"

I nodded. "Yep! I know we originally agreed to the possibility of having Micah come stay the weekend with us, but I figured you needed some time to yourself after all the hard work you've been doing. And I knew the only people you'd trust to watch Micah overnight like that would be Will and Sadie. So I thought you'd prefer that over the nanny."

But, she wasn't smiling the way I thought she would have been.

"Is that... not a good thing?" I asked.

Ellie's gaze fell to her lap. "I just wish you would've asked me about that before going behind my back and making plans for my son, that's all."

I winced at the harshness of her words. "Look, Ellie, nothing has to happen this weekend. If you want, I can text Sadie right now and—"

She held her hand up. "Anything concerning my son can be done through me but thank you."

Fuck. "Yeah, yeah. Of course. I'm—I'm sorry, Ellie. I just thought it would've been nice for the two of us to have a bit of time together without you having to worry about so much. I guess I didn't fully think it through."

And when she didn't say anything, I knew I had fucked up royally.

Great. Way to be a typical guy, Ryan.

When I saw Ellie stand and toss her napkin onto the table, I figured this was it. She'd ask me to take her home and the entire weekend would be ruined. I couldn't blame her, though. I had pulled a very dick move and overstepped my boundaries in ways I hadn't earned yet.

However, what she did was very different from what I thought she was going to do.

I stood to my feet. "Ellie, I'm so sorry. I just thought that—"

She gripped my suit jacket. "Shut up and kiss me, Ryan."

Ellie pulled me into her, and our lips crashed together, like waves of an ocean defying all matters of natural order to find one another. And the second our tongues fell together, lightning shot through my body. Fireworks went off in my head as she melted against me, her body flush with mine. I cloaked her spine with my arms, cradling her as her pillowy lips massaged my own. I growled down the back of her throat. I dipped her back and felt her giggle before I swallowed the sound whole.

"Ahem."

The waitress clearing her throat pierced through our moment, and Ellie started giggling. I stood her up onto her feet and tucked a stray strand of hair behind her ear before cupping her cheek. And after she kissed the tip of my nose, our waitress walked up.

"Whenever you two are ready, I can take your order," she said.

Ellie smiled. "Thank you for this."

I nodded. "It's the absolute least you deserve after how hard you work for you and your son."

Her eyes watered over. "It's hard for me to let go sometimes, especially when Micah doesn't have his father around."

"Makes you feel guilty for going and enjoying time by yourself, doesn't it?"

She nodded a bit. "Sometimes, yeah."

I peeked over at the waitress. "Bring us one of everything on our procured menu. Including desserts. We might as well try them all."

The waitress smiled. "One of everything coming up."

I gazed back into Ellie's eyes. "Care to sit and have your fill of wonderful food?"

She slid her fingertip down my tie. "I think I'd like my fill of something else before the food gets here."

I quirked an eyebrow. "Why, Miss Ellie, are you suggesting...?"

Her hand fell to my belt buckle. "That's exactly what I'm suggesting."

I couldn't sit down quickly enough as she pressed my knees apart with her hands. She knelt between my legs, licking those lips of hers as the tablecloth draped over her head. Her hands slid up my thighs when I pulled out my cock, stroking it as it grew thicker and thicker. And as I kept my eye on the kitchen door, ready to hide her at a second's notice, she wrapped her lips around the tip of my dick and then slid it all the way to the back of her fucking throat.

"Good God," I growled.

She pulled the tablecloth over her head and my exposed hips, completely covering herself in case someone walked in. And as she played with my balls, her tongue traced the bulging vein on the underside of my cock. I shivered with delight as I curled my fingers tightly into her tendrils. I bucked against her face, feeling her nose caressing my trimmed hair. And the tighter she sucked, the more my toes curled in my shoes.

"Mmm," she hummed.

And the vibrations sent my body through the fucking roof.

As I swallowed my grunts and my growls, my balls pulled up into my body. My hips left the seat of the chair as Ellie swallowed me whole, opening up her throat for my pleasure. My thighs quivered as my arousal shot from the tip of my cock, coating her mouth and sliding effortlessly down the back of her throat.

I collapsed against the chair, spent and panting for air, as she released my dick from her throat. She giggled and kissed my dwindling girth, her fingernails teasing the inside of my thighs.

Then, she crawled underneath the table to her chair and popped up as if nothing had ever happened.

And I sat there with the tablecloth covering my naked pelvis as the waitress came out with our first round of appetizers.

22

Ellie

Dinner was a wonderful affair of lustful glances, rich red wines, and platefuls of decadent food that I stuffed myself to the brim with. Everything tasted fantastic, from the bruschetta to the house-made pasta to the fresh sauces to all of the desserts we got to pick at and try. I had no idea how much this evening had cost Ryan, but I'd make sure he got his money's worth before I had my fill of him all weekend.

I giggled at the way he couldn't speak for a while. Every time the waitress talked to him, he had to clear his throat and squint to focus. It was the cutest thing I'd ever witnessed in my life, and all I wanted was to make him feel like that all weekend. My heart soared with delight at every bite he fed me from across the table. My stomach jutted out with all of the food we stuffed down in there. And by the time Ryan paid the bill, I was ready to get out of my heels and this dress before getting into Ryan's pants again.

The ride to the hotel was silent. Ryan held my hand tightly, our fingers intertwined as he parked the truck. He was a true gentleman, opening doors for me and escorting me all the way to the hotel suite with his hand on the small of my back.

But, nothing prepared me for the decadence behind the door as we walked inside.

"What in the world?" I asked breathlessly.

I had never once seen vaulted ceilings in a hotel room before, but this one had them. The exposed beams were stained a dark, rich wood color, and it really brought out the whites of the walls. There was a set of French doors that led out onto our own private balcony, and the king-size bed in the open-concept studio room sat inside a four-poster frame with sheer curtain-like fabrics draping from the rafters. The plush carpet beneath my heels made me feel as if I were walking on a cloud. There was a jetted tub and a massive stand-up shower in the bathroom, and my mind immediately filled with all of the salacious things we could get up to in those alone.

"Ryan, this place is amazing," I whispered.

I slowly turned to face him and found his tie loosened. His suit jacket, unbuttoned. His hands, already sliding his belt out of their loops. His eyes darkened with a desperate need that I felt churning in my gut, and as he stalked toward me, I braced myself for the inevitable.

"Ryan!" I squealed.

"Come here, gorgeous." Then he scooped me into his arms, threw me over his shoulder, and spanked my ass.

I kicked my feet until my heels came off. "Ryan! Put me down!"

He spanked my ass again. "As you wish." He tossed me onto the bed, and my entire body bounced for his viewing pleasure.

And by the time I got settled onto the mattress, he was naked for me. His muscles, chiseled and strong. Flexing for me and bulging with veins that my tongue wanted to trace.

"Ryan," I whispered.

He knelt onto the mattress. "Spread those legs wide for me, beautiful. I haven't had my fill of dessert just yet."

My panties didn't even come off. All he did was fall forward and slide them to the side before diving between my soaked pussy lips. And it didn't take long for me to start chanting his name. My eyes screwed themselves shut as I bucked against his face, ravenously chasing my end. His fingers filled me. His body overtook my own. His growling voice rattled my ribcage and sent me soaring into the dark-stained wooden rafters.

"Ryan, please! I'm so fucking close!" And when his tongue flattened out over my clit, I lost myself in a euphoric abyss. "Yes. Yes. Oh, holy shit, yes," I gasped.

He raced up my body and crushed our lips together, his

hands pawing at my clothes to get them off. We rolled around, casting off my outfit piece by piece until nothing came between us. I kissed him until my lips hurt. I licked my juices off his face, enjoying the taste of myself against his sun-kissed skin.

And when he slid his cock inside of me with one fell swoop, the words fell from my lips like rainwater from a gutter. "I love you. I love you so much, Ryan."

He pounded into me as my breasts jumped against his chest. He covered my mouth with his own, his tongue invading me as his cock slid against every beautiful sweet spot I had inside my body. I dragged my nails down his back as the frame of the bed knocked against the wall. I felt my juices dripping down my ass crack just before he flipped me over and pulled my hips into the air.

And as he entered me from behind, I heard those fatal words. Words that sealed our fate together before he spanked my ass again. "I love you, too. Good Christ, I love you so much."

I pressed back against him as his cock grew bigger inside of me. I cried out in ecstasy against the comforter, muting my sounds as bliss rushed through my veins. My eyes rolled into the back of my head. I felt yet another orgasm coming on. And when I popped, my walls spasmed around him, pulling him over the edge with me.

"Oh, shit. There it is. There it is, Ellie. Fuck. I love you. Yeah, grip that dick. You like that?"

I whimpered through the spiraling darkness. "Yes. Ryan, oh my *God.*"

He collapsed against my back, sending me tumbling onto the mattress stomach-first. He panted against my shoulder as his cock filled me to the brim before my pussy pushed him out. The evidence of our climaxes leaked against the sheets. I felt the proof of our debauchery, coating the sheets beneath my body. And when Ryan rolled off me, he wrapped me in his arms and dragged me with him and right out of the mess we had created together.

"Jesus, Ellie," he said breathlessly.

I tossed my arm over my eyes. "Holy fuck, that was outstanding."

His fingertips traced faceless designs against my stomach. "Did you mean it?"

My arm fell away from my eyes, and I turned my head so he could see the truth in my stare. "Yeah. Did you?"

He kissed the back of my head. "I have for a while now. Just took me a bit of time to realize it and a little longer to voice it."

I heard something ding in the distance, and Ryan quickly shifted. I groaned as he moved off the bed and padded to the foot of it, digging through the pile of his clothes. I watched him hold his phone up to his face, squinting as if he couldn't see the lit-up screen well enough.

Then, the look on his face completely shifted.

Something's wrong. "What is it, Ryan?"

He quickly texted something back before turning his attention to me. "What was that, beautiful?"

I covered myself with the sheet. "You look like something's wrong. Who texted you?"

He brought his phone over to his bedside table. "It's just something wor—" He cut off his own sentence, and I sat up.

I placed my back against the headboard as he eased himself onto the edge of the couch. There was a war going on behind his eyes, and it killed me to watch it play out. I reached over and settled my hand on top of his, trying to comfort him as much as possible.

Then, as he looked up into my eyes, a knot formed in my stomach. "Whatever it is, you might as well blurt it out. We're kind of in head-deep as it is."

He snickered. "I suppose you're right."

"I'll tell my secret if you tell yours?"

He cocked his head. "You'll really tell me what you're hiding if I'm simply honest?"

I shrugged. "The mere fact that you know I'm not telling you something tells me I'm not hiding it as well as I thought I was. So, might as well, right?"

He laced our fingers together. "Remember when I said I wanted a big family?"

I nodded slowly, hoping our perfect little world wasn't about to burst. "Yeah, I do."

"Well, before we struck this thing up between us, I kind of..."

I scooted closer to him. "Trust me, it can't be any worse

than my secret, Ryan. Just say it. Give it life so we can talk about it."

He sighed. "The ding was a large sum of money leaving my checking account. I get alerts every time they happen."

"Oh? Did you buy something?"

He scoffed. "I mean, it was a down payment for something, kind of. Yeah."

"Well, that isn't too bad. What did you buy? A massive van for all of your future children?"

He swallowed hard. "Kinda gotta have the children first."

I blinked. "I'm not following."

He turned his body toward me. "The money leaving my account was for a surrogate I hired to have my first child."

His words took me out at the knees. It reminded me of what I couldn't give him, and at that moment, I knew I couldn't stay. I loved this man more than my own life. At some point in time, my crush on him had become the real deal, and I couldn't stick by him knowing I couldn't provide for him the one thing he was this desperate to seek out for himself. I squeezed his hand and blinked back tears. I swallowed the knot forming in my throat as he looked away from me.

"It's nothing to be ashamed of, Ryan. You want a family, and you're giving yourself that. I think it's wonderful," I said.

"But?" he asked as his eyes came back to mine.

I slid my hand away. "But, I can't be with you knowing this."

He snickered. "You're kidding, right?"

I slid to the other side of the bed. "Trust me, it's for the best. Because if you're going to a surrogate to have a family, then that tells me exactly how much you want children of your own."

I eased myself off the mattress and started gathering my clothes. I felt Ryan's eyes on me as I pulled my panties up my legs and tugged my dress over my head. I felt my heart shattering into a million pieces as I got dressed. But, when I started fluffing my hair around my shoulders, preparing to take my leave, he spoke and his words froze me in my tracks.

"If the surrogacy is going to stand in the way of us, I'll cancel."

I peered over my shoulder. "That would be like asking a pregnant woman to get an abortion because a child doesn't suit her current predicament. I'm not going to ask you to do that."

He stood to his feet. "We haven't even gone to the egg donation center yet. She's not pregnant. I have a right to cancel at any time, and I'm more than willing to do that if it means getting a chance with you."

A tear slipped down my cheek. "Ryan, I have to go."

He rushed around the bed and took my hands in his. "Ellie, just listen to me. I want you. All of you. Every single part of you and Micah. I want to be in your life, in whatever capacity you'll have me. But I really love this particular capacity. I want us to be in *this* capacity."

I pulled away from him. "Ryan, trust me, this is for the

best. What you want and what I'm capable of giving are two very different things."

He cupped my cheeks. "Then talk to me, Ellie! Just talk! That's all I'm asking you to do, just like you asked me!"

I shoved him away. "I can't talk about it because it hurts, okay?"

He held out his arms. "And you don't think this is hurting me right now? At least I gave us a chance to try to figure things out. You're making a decision about my life without giving me any input. How is that not supposed to hurt?"

"We're talking about the future of your family here, Ryan. The children that you want!"

"Yeah, Ellie. And I'd love for you to be their mother. Can't you see that?"

I started shrieking, I was so angry. "Well, I can't be their fucking mother, Ryan, because I can't fucking have any more children in the first goddamn place, so why the fuck am I still standing here, arguing with you?"

And the second the words flew out of my mouth, I knew I was screwed. The second I saw Ryan's face contort into one of confusion, I knew we were fucked.

Why the hell did my ex have to ruin my entire life in one fell swoop?

❧ 23 ❧

Ryan

Her words settled against my mind once I was able to tear them away from the tone of her voice, and my heart broke. Not because of her words, though, but because of Ellie's tears. I remembered back to all of the times I mentioned to her that I wanted a large family one day, and the idea of those words hurting her every single time killed something inside of me. I watched her collapse back onto the bed in a fit of tears and trembling. I rushed to her side and wrapped her up in my arms, bringing her wet face to the crook of my neck.

And as she continued to speak, my heart continued to ache for her. "I can't have your children, Ryan. I don't even have a fucking uterus anymore. I–I–I–I can't give you what you want. A–a–and–and you deserve what you want. You're so amazing, a–a–and so awesome and so wonderful and loving. And you just deserve the whole world, and I can't give it to you, and I'm sorry, but that's why I have to leave. That's why we can't do this."

I kissed the top of her head. "Shut up and calm down so we can talk about this. I'm not going anywhere, all right?"

She sniffled. "Don't tell me to shut up."

I chuckled. "Then, don't start making decisions about my life based on information I don't have. Nothing makes me angrier quicker."

She sobbed harder. "I'm so sorry, Ryan."

I scooped her into my lap. "It's okay. Get it out, and when you're good again, we can talk."

I rocked her side to side, shushing her softly against the shell of her ear. I told her it would be okay, and that I wasn't going anywhere, and that I was proud of her for finally telling me, for finally trusting me with something like that, even if she did yell it out of desperation. I stroked my fingers through her knotted hair as her crying eventually dried up. I wiped some of the tears off her cheek as she nestled deeply against my body. I never wanted Ellie to be this upset about something ever again. I never wanted to argue like that, or yell like that, or speak to one another like that.

"You ready to talk?" I murmured.

And when she sat up, I placed her back against the mattress so I could look straight into her eyes. "Ellie, look at me."

Her eyes connected with mine. "I'm sorry for yelling."

I tucked a strand of hair behind her ear. "So am I. It was uncalled for on both sides."

She wiped at her tears. "I can't give you a family, Ryan."

I shrugged. "Good thing there's more than one way to have a kid."

She blinked. "What?"

I gripped her chin. "Ellie, do you want more kids?"

"I can't have more kids."

"That's not what I asked. In general, do you *want* more kids?"

She nodded slowly. "Yeah. I do. I mean, I'm an only child, and the only family I have left is Sadie. I don't want Micah's life to be like mine."

I kissed her forehead. "Then, that's all that matters. The rest, we can figure out along the way."

"But—you don't want your own kids?"

I shrugged. "Just because you can't physically carry kids doesn't mean I can't have biological children. Why do you think I'm going the surrogacy route?"

She sighed. "I don't even have eggs, Ryan. I mean, I had a few frozen just on a whim after the surgery, but I don't know if—"

"Ellie, calm down."

She drew in a deep breath. "I can't ask you to compromise your future family for me."

"And I'm not. You're not listening to me, and I need you to listen to my words. There is more than one way to have a child nowadays. There's adoption, and surrogacy with egg donation banks, and taking your frozen eggs with my sperm and implanting it into someone else. Ellie, families don't have to be traditional to be families. Just look at me and all of my brothers."

She giggled. "Your family tree is pretty intricate, yeah."

"Exactly. Because there's no one right way to have a family."

She closed her eyes. "Micah's birth was just so traumatic, and—"

I pulled her against my side and tucked her underneath my arm. "Wanna talk about it?"

She paused. "Actually, yeah. I kind of do. With you, at least."

I kissed the top of her head. "Then, I'm all ears, beautiful."

She drew in a deep breath. "My pregnancy with Micah wasn't the easiest. I mean, I had bleeding on and off that always took me to the emergency room, and there were a couple of times where my OB was concerned about the placement of my placenta. But, I mean, it was all manageable, you know?"

I rubbed my hand up and down her arm as she gathered the strength to continue.

"But then I went into early labor. Not too early, but about five weeks ahead of schedule. The doctors tried to stop my labor before they realized I was too far along, and all of that medication kind of fucked with me, I guess. I pushed for hours before Micah finally came out, but the problem was that the placenta had detached too early, I guess? So, it all kind of came out at once."

"What happened after that?" I asked.

She shook her head. "It's all such a blur. I remember feeling kind of loopy and Micah crying. I remember his crying fading away and wheels squeaking. And then, the next thing I know, I'm in a recovery room from surgery, and the doctor is telling me that Micah is okay and I'm going to be okay; it was all just so much."

I turned her eyes up to mine. "What happened?"

She licked her chapped lips. "Micah got the cord wrapped around his throat, and because my placenta was already weak —or so they said—his birth caused him to pull the placenta along with him. He was okay, but the placenta ripped a part of the inside of my uterus off with it, so I started bleeding out right after Micah arrived."

"Good God," I whispered.

She shrugged. "The doctor said there was so much blood loss that the only thing that saved my life was a full hysterectomy. And even then, I needed three units of blood before I was strong enough to see Micah and feed him."

I wiped the rest of the tears off her cheeks. "I'm so fucking sorry, Ellie. And I'm so sorry you had to do it alone."

She shook her head. "Oh, I wasn't alone. I mean, I didn't have Micah's father there, no. But, Sadie was there. Sadie was there the whole time, and I'll never be able to thank her enough for it."

I slid my fingers through her hair. "How are you feeling?"

She heaved a heavy sigh. "Drained."

I chuckled. "Ready for the kicker in all this?"

She closed her eyes once more. "Yeah, go ahead."

I snickered. "That still doesn't prevent us from having the family we both want."

She leaned against me. "I don't know how you came into my life or what I did to deserve you but thank you for choosing me."

I kissed the top of her head. "I didn't have a choice. You sank your talons into me the first time our eyes ever connected. I'm yours until you tell me otherwise."

Our fingers threaded together before I eased us back against the bed. And as we lay there, staring up at the ceiling, a smile crept across my face. Yes, I was broken-hearted for Ellie's predicament. But, we'd just had our first fight as a couple in love, and we came out on the other side of it reasonably unscathed.

"We have some things to work on, but I give it a six out of ten," I said.

Ellie froze. "What?"

I looked over at her. "Our first argument. There was a bit more yelling in the beginning than I would have wished, but we still came back together and talked it out. Overall, six out of ten. Would've been an eight had we not had the yelling."

She blinked. "You're insane, you know that?"

I rolled myself on top of her. "Does that mean you're

going to take these dreaded clothes off and stay at least one night with me?"

"Do you really still want me after all of that?"

I shrugged. "Why not? I love you, you love me. We're kind of stuck until one of us gets fed up with the other."

She cupped my cheek. "Thank you for such a lovely night. I'm sorry that I ruined it."

I kissed her lips softly. "You didn't ruin anything. Though, given what we just talked about, I'm not so sure this is the weekend for us to spend time alone in a hotel room."

"What do you mean?"

I stood and took her hands in mine before helping her to her feet. "You went through a lot to have Micah. And now that I have the ball rolling with my surrogate, it's only going to be a matter of time before we've got two kiddos to keep up with. And while I'd love to enjoy this weekend completely naked with you, something in the pit of my gut tells me we should both be spending this time with Micah. Don't you think?"

She smiled. "I don't know if I can love you more than I do right now."

I grinned. "I'm sure it's possible, and I'll find all of the ways I can in order to prove it to you."

She threw her arms around my neck and kissed me with a fiery need that set my heart aflame. I cradled her in my arms, tasting the saltiness of her tears as her tongue slid against my own. I loved this woman with everything inside of me, and if we were really going to do this, then I needed to form my own relationship with Micah before my own little one eventually came along.

So, we got dressed, said goodbye to the hotel room, and started back down to my truck.

With our fingers intertwined and our hearts synced as one, I watched as she used her free hand to text Sadie. Will would have plenty of questions for me come morning, which meant I needed to avoid him at all costs. I didn't want to be speaking about anything regarding Ellie and what had happened tonight without her explicit consent.

But, as I walked her to her front door, it hit me. "What are you and Micah doing for breakfast in the morning?" I asked.

Ellie unlocked her front door. "Uh, well. Saturday mornings, I usually throw a little something together. Which typically ends up with Micah eating cheesy scrambled eggs while I down half a pot of caffeine."

I smirked. "So, if I were to bring breakfast from, say, Linead's tomorrow, you wouldn't turn it down?"

She blinked. "Linead's?"

"Uh-huh."

"You mean that wonderful place Sadie and the girls take me to sometimes for brunch?"

I nodded. "That's the one."

Her eyes lit up. "Can we get their pancakes? Ugh, I've never had better pancakes than I've had from there. Micah would love a peanut butter one alongside his cheesy scrambled eggs."

I kissed her lips softly. "You text me whatever the two of you want, and I'll be here around eight with the food."

She cupped my cheek. "Can you make it seven-thirty? Micah gets up around seven and usually gives me about half an hour before he's complaining about his tummy."

"Hey, I'm not one to deny a growing boy. I'll be here promptly at seven-thirty, then."

She shook her head. "God, you're perfect. You know that?"

I slid my thumb across her cheek. "Perfect for you, just like you're perfect for me." I bent to capture her lips, leaving so much to be desired as I pulled away. I let my eyes fall down her body one last time before I shook my head, and that caused her to giggle.

"Don't worry, we'll have plenty of time alone once Micah goes down for his nap after lunch tomorrow," she said.

I took a step back. "So, I'm staying for more than just breakfast?"

She leaned against her open doorway. "Might as well, right?"

I winked at her. "Might as well, gorgeous."

My back fell against my truck before she turned and walked inside. She peeked out the door one last time before closing it, and I had half a mind to follow her inside and take her one last time against one of those living room windows. But, I resisted the urge and instead climbed up into my truck. My brothers would have plenty of questions for me whenever

I saw them next, and I needed to brace myself for disappointing them with my answers.

But until then, I had the best woman on the planet at my side while we navigated a path that was new for both of us.

A path I hoped we continued down for the rest of our lives.

❧ 24 ❧

Ellie

I woke up to the incredible smell of butter on pancakes, and my son giggling down the hallway. But, as soon as his giggling hit my ears, I shot right out of bed. I scrambled to pick up my phone as it dropped to the floor, and when the screen lit up, I gasped.

Holy shit, it's nine in the morning.

"Micah!" I exclaimed.

"Mommy, eggs!"

I stumbled around for my robe. "I'm coming to make you some! I—"

Wait, why is he not in his room?

"Ellie, don't panic. I'm here in the kitchen." Ryan's voice fluttered down the hallway, and I paused.

In my sleepy haze and non-caffeinated state, I could have sworn Micah was out there with Ryan. But that wasn't possible, right?

"How—how did you get—?"

Ryan peeked around the corner into my bedroom. "I had Bryce let me in. When I knocked and you didn't answer, I figured either something was wrong, or you were still sleeping."

I ran my hand through my knotted hair. "Right, right."

He thumbed over his shoulder. "Got a hot mug of coffee for you and pancakes I just warmed up. You want butter and syrup on them?"

I nodded slowly. "Was—was Micah up when you—?"

He walked into the room and cupped my cheeks. "Don't worry. He's in his highchair eating a second helping of eggs and wolfing down some peanut butter pancakes like the growing boy he is."

I sighed. "I can't remember the last time I slept this late."

He kissed my lips softly. "Just because we aren't in a hotel doesn't mean I can't treat you to a late morning. Come on, Micah's been asking for you for a few minutes now."

I walked out into the hallway with Ryan and smiled at the sound of my son yelling for me through a mouthful of food. I walked into the kitchen and kissed him on his disheveled little head and listened as he giggled with delight. He took a massive handful of eggs and shoved them into his mouth, acting as if I didn't feed him four times a day with snacks.

And when I sat down, a plate of delicious food appeared in front of me. "Oh, wow," I whispered.

Ryan slid my coffee toward me. "Figured you might want that first."

I reached for the mug. "And you'd be right."

I sipped my coffee, trying to wake up, as I watched Ryan wipe the eggs off of Micah's face. I watched as he made his own plate of food while doting on my son and talking back to him whenever Micah addressed him. It was the cutest thing in the world to witness, and the smile on my son's face was one I'd never seen before.

It made me feel like the guiltiest parent in the world. But, it also gave me hope for mine and Ryan's future.

"So, how did you sleep last night?" he asked.

Micah stabbed at his hash browns before shoving them into his face with his hands. Then Ryan handed Micah his fork, helping him get a few hash browns on the prongs before putting them into his mouth. My eyes widened as Micah giggled with delight, slamming his fork against the plastic high chair tray in front of him.

"I can barely get him to use that thing half the time," I said breathlessly.

Ryan chuckled. "Well, maybe you shouldn't always eat with your hands, then."

I shot him a look. "I'm not that caffeinated yet."

He held his hands up. "I surrender! I surrender!"

Micah threw his head back with laughter. "Surremmer! Surremmer!"

I couldn't help but giggle with wide eyes as he looked over at Ryan. The two of them smiled at one another and, dammit, I wished I would have had my phone accessible to take a picture. I'd never seen my son take to someone like this before. I mean, hell, Micah had been around Will all of his life, and he hadn't bonded like this with him. It was hard to get Micah to say three or four words to me some days, the kid was so shy.

Yet here he was, laughing with Ryan as if they were the best of friends.

I finally found you.

"You gonna eat?" Ryan asked.

I drew in a deep breath and looked down at my plate. "Don't you even think about touching my food. That's my food."

Micah giggled. "Mommy likes food."

Ryan snickered. "And it's one of the many things I like about her."

I finally dove into my breakfast, but there was something Ryan had said last night that kept spinning around in my head. And while I wasn't sure if breakfast in front of Micah was an appropriate time to bring it up, I didn't want too much time to pass by before I mentioned it.

So, I drew in a deep breath. "You're a good man, you know that?"

Ryan's eyes met mine. "Thank you. I appreciate that, Ellie."

"And it's clear to me from the bit of time you've spent

with Micah that you're kind of a natural at all of this."

"I've always loved kids."

I nodded. "Which is why I hope you haven't already canceled things with your surrogate."

He blinked. "Really?"

I smiled softly. "Really, really. Ryan, don't put those kinds of plans off just because of what you might believe I'm thinking. If this is something you want, I know in the pit of my gut you're going to be a wonderful father, and I can't rob you of something like that. I'd never forgive myself."

He took my hand from across the table. "So, it's okay with you if I proceed with things?"

I shrugged. "Hey, I've got a kid. You help me with mine, and I'll help you with yours."

He blinked. "So, does this mean I can take you out again?"

I smiled brightly. "Yes. Especially if it means you continuously bring over breakfasts the next morning. We could get used to eating like this."

Micah's voice soared over our heads. "More eggs, pwease!"

My eyebrows shot up my forehead. "Since when do you use manners?"

Ryan chuckled as he stood. "Since I told him that all good boys use manners. And he wants to be a good boy, right?"

Micah nodded vigorously. "Uh-huh. Good boy, always."

I reached out and cupped my son's cheek. "I love you so much. You know that?"

He nodded. "Love oo, too."

"So!" Ryan said as he retrieved more food for my bottomless pit of a child, "how do you feel about going out again tonight? I don't want to ruin your weekend jive, but I kind of did make reservations at this Greek place I thought you might enjoy."

"Mmm, Greek food sounds amazing."

He gave Micah his food and sat back down. "Yeah, they even have one of those spits that they carve the meat from right in front of you. I've heard it's a real trip."

I started searching for my cell phone. "I mean, I'd have to call Sadie, but..."

He pulled out his phone. "I've got Will's number. Want me to call him?"

I nodded. "Yeah, and just tell him to give the phone to Sadie."

"Can do."

He dialed the number and promptly told Will to hand the phone to his "baby mama," then gave the phone to me. I snickered and shook my head as I heard shuffling around on the other end of the line, then Sadie's voice appeared groggily in my ear.

"Yeah, Ryan?"

I giggled. "Rise and shine, beautiful."

She drew in a deep breath. "And I was sleeping so *good*."

"You can go back to sleep after I ask you to watch Micah tonight so Ryan and I can go out again. Apparently, we're getting Greek."

I heard her shuffling around some more. "Aren't you supposed to be in a hotel right now or something?" She must really be out of it since I had explained all of this to her last night when I had picked up Micah.

Will yelled in the background. "Did he fuck it up?"

I barked with laughter. "No, Will. He didn't fuck it up."

Ryan rolled his eyes before taking another bite of his food.

"Anyway, would that be okay? Or, should we cancel the reservations?" I asked.

Sadie yawned. "Hey, I'm down for it. We were supposed to have him tonight anyway with the original plans. Any reason why you guys decided against the hotel room? I kind of thought maybe you'd take Micah back with you tonight."

I shrugged. "We just didn't feel it was the right time in our relationship to be doing something like that."

She squealed like a giddy little schoolgirl. "Oh. My. God. Are you two a couple now?"

Will yelled again in the background. "You owe me fifty bucks, Sadie!"

"Shut up! I'm talking here!" she exclaimed.

I clapped my hand over my mouth to keep from bursting out laughing. Sadie and Will went back and forth for a little bit, and I thought about when Ryan and I might get to that point. The idea of waking up to him every morning made me smile. The idea of spending every non-caffeinated breakfast with him made my heart take flight. I looked over at him from across the table and found him smiling at me, and I knew that smile was the one I wanted to see for the rest of my life.

"So? What's the verdict? Are you two an item, or what?" Sadie asked.

I held Ryan's stare. "Yeah, Ryan and I are in a relationship."

And the massive smile that peeled across his cheeks sent my heart thundering with joyous bliss.

"Girl, of course, we can take Micah. He's welcome anytime. But, Will wants me to tell you that you guys now owe us a weekend alone."

I nodded. "Ryan and I are more than willing to foot that exchange. A weekend of dates for a weekend of dates."

Ryan pointed his fork at me. "It's only fair."

I held out my hand. "See? I don't know if you heard him, but he agrees."

Sadie squealed this time. "Yay! I've been wanting to plan this little spa retreat for Will and me, but I can't pull him away from home long enough. The man's more domesticated than I am!"

Will shouted from somewhere in the background. "I heard that!"

Sadie yelled back, "Good, ya old fart!"

I laughed until tears rushed my eyes, and my stomach hurt. Micah started giggling along with me, and pretty soon, all of us were laughing up a storm—it felt so good. It felt so amazing to be this happy with my life. And when I heard my business email notification trill down the hallway, I knew my day was about to get that much better.

"All right, all right, all right. I have to give Ryan his phone back. But, we'll drop Micah off around...?"

Ryan whispered, "Five."

"How's five sound, Sadie?"

I heard her throw the covers off her body. "Five sounds fine. And seriously, girl, don't feel bad about him staying the night. It's totally okay if that's where the date takes you guys."

I smiled. "I think I might feel a little bit better about that now, so I might just take you up on that offer."

"Good, because you deserve it."

"Thank you. I appreciate it so much. Here, I'm handing you back to Ryan."

"I'll go ahead and hang up, then. Tell Ryan I said not to fuck it up!"

I covered the receiver with my hand. "Sadie says not to screw it up tonight."

Ryan held the keycard for the hotel suite up. "You just say the word, okay?"

My eyes widened. "You didn't cancel the hotel?"

He shrugged. "Can't. Already bought and paid for."

"Well, we're using it tonight, so be prepared."

He grinned wildly. "I'm always prepared."

Sadie yelled in my ear, "Love you, girl. Gotta go! Bye!"

I smiled. "Love you, too, Sadie. Bye-bye!"

I handed Ryan his phone back and slipped back into enjoying a great meal with the two most important men in my life. Micah filled his stomach twice over before he and Ryan started talking and babbling at one another, and it warmed my heart so much I thought I might burst. We talked, and we laughed. We cracked jokes and made plans for the rest of our evening. I talked to Micah about how he was going to sleep over with the twins, and I'd never seen him so excited about being away from me.

It tugged at my heart a little bit to know my boy was growing up and becoming independent.

But then again, that was what children did.

"I love you, Ellie," Ryan said.

My eyes came back to his, and I smiled. "I love you, too, Ryan."

He stood and came around to my side of the table before offering me his hand. I took it, and he pulled me to my feet as he wrapped his arms around my waist. My hands pressed against his chest. I gazed up into his eyes as he rocked me gently from side to side, almost as if we were dancing in the living room.

Maybe one day we will actually be man and wife.

But, I kept that little tidbit to myself.

Instead, I kissed his chest softly and rested my ear against his beating heart. With my son banging his fork against his tray with eggs all over his face and in his hair, I closed my eyes and listened as Ryan hummed a little musical tune just for us to hear. We swayed back and forth, my arms tightly wrapped around him as he cradled me against his chest.

And with every rock of our bodies, images of our future bombarded my mind.

I saw our children rallying around us as I cooked breakfast

every morning. I saw Ryan kissing me as I went off to work, banging out beautiful iron and metal sculptures for people to put in their yards. I saw a massive two-story home with a wrap-around porch sitting by a beautiful pond, with two swing sets out back and horses off in the distance.

Somehow, this impossible man happened to be made just for me.

And I wouldn't have had it any other way.

EPILOGUE

Ryan
One Year Later

Leslie cried out in pain as she squeezed my hand. The doctor between her legs kept coaching her through her pushing. And when I looked over at Ellie dabbing sweat off our surrogate's forehead, I knew our lives as we understood them were about to change.

"Come on, Leslie. You've got this. Take a deep breath and push as hard as you can," Ellie said.

Leslie bared down. "Holy fucki—*agh*!"

I grunted. "Holy hell, that's a grip."

Ellie wiped the sweat off Leslie's brow again. "Want some ice?"

Leslie nodded. "Please."

The doctor intervened. "No ice. Not right now. We need her focused."

Ellie snapped her head around. "If she wants ice to make her feel better, that's what I'm going to give her. It's not enough that this system starves women in the middle of labor, so you're gonna take away her ice, too?"

I looked down at the doctor. "They understand the risks. Just go with it."

He nodded. "All right, on the count of three, Leslie. One, two—"

Leslie groaned. "Holy shit, she's *coming!*"

Ellie laughed with joy. "That's it. You've got this. Come on, girl! Let 'er rip!"

Everything happened so quickly that it almost became a blur. I looked around, trying to take it all in. Leslie collapsed back against the pillow, and I watched my beautiful fiancée feed her little ice chips. I saw the doctors and the nurses scrambling between our surrogate's legs before handing the doctor blankets and scissors. My eyes widened as he held my sweet, beautiful daughter up for my eyes to see.

Then, a nurse tapped me on the shoulder. "Want to do the honors, Dad?"

My eyes welled with tears. "Ellie?"

She giggled. "I did it with my son. You do this with your daughter, sweetheart."

I looked over at her. "Our daughter, Ellie. This is *our* daughter, remember?"

She smiled at me with tears trickling down her cheeks

before she nodded and came over. She handed Leslie the ice chips as I positioned the scissors right where the doctor told us to cut. Then, Ellie placed her hand over mine, and we snipped our daughter's umbilical cord together. Listening to our sweet baby girl cry was one of the most beautiful, most heart-wrenching moments of my life. I never wanted the women in my life to cry, and this sweet bundle of joy was no different.

For as long as I lived, I'd do anything to see my family smile.

"She's perfect," Ellie whispered.

The doctor handed our daughter to her mother, and I rushed back up to dote on Leslie. I didn't want her to feel as if she had been forgotten, but the second I tried smoothing her hair away from her face, Leslie shooed me away.

"Go be with your little girl, just go get my husband," she whispered.

And after I kissed her hand, I did exactly as she asked.

There was a lot of shuffling about as we made our leave. The nurses ushered us into a fresh "mommy-baby suite" where we'd stay for a couple of days just to make sure things were okay before going home. I felt terrible that we had to leave Leslie in that room by herself. But, as we rushed down the hallway, I saw her husband running for us.

"How'd it go?" he called out.

I smiled. "She's great. They're both great. Leslie's asking for you."

He patted my shoulder. "Thanks, man."

I gripped his arm, stopping him in his tracks. "No. Thank you. I'll never be able to thank you and your wife enough for what you've done for Ellie and me."

We embraced in a hug as the nurses continued to rush Ellie and our daughter off. But, once we released one another, the delivery doctor ushered me into the room we were to occupy for a couple of nights. I walked into the beautiful sight of Ellie rocking our baby girl in her arms while staring down into her sweet, little face. And when she reached for our baby's first bottle, I reveled at how tiny it was. The damn thing was no bigger than my thumb. Shit, the nipple head was bigger than the bottle itself!

"How is everything? What do you need?" I asked softly.

Ellie smiled up at me. "Come hold your daughter's hand while she eats. It's how you can bond with her."

I walked over gingerly and peeked over the edge of my little girl's hat. And when her eyes looked straight up into mine, I noticed they were the same color eyes as Ellie's. Tears rushed my eyes as I reached out my finger, searching for her hand.

And when our little girl slid her arm out to wrap her tiny little hand around my finger, a tear fell from my eye.

"You're perfect, April," I whispered.

Ellie giggled. "April Lee?"

I kissed April's forehead. "April Lee Remington, it is."

The massive diamond on Ellie's left hand sparkled in the sunlight that streamed through the window. I pulled up a chair and watched as our little girl drained her bottle.

But, instead of Ellie burping her, she stood to her feet. "Take off your shirt."

I blinked. "What?"

She giggled. "You're going to burp April, but you should do it skin to skin. That also helps with bonding."

I nodded. "Yeah, yeah. I can do that."

I quickly stood up and slipped off my shirt before Ellie handed me our little girl. I cradled her softly against my shoulder and lightly tapped her back, hoping and praying I wasn't being too rough.

"You can do it a little harder than that. She really needs some nice pats before—"

Ellie didn't even get finished with her statement before I gave April a harder tap. And when I did, I felt something wet against my skin as she let out the biggest burp I'd ever heard come out of a child.

"Holy shit, what was that?" I asked.

Ellie picked up my shirt and giggled. "See? She had gas, but she spit up a bit on you. Hold on."

As I watched her clean off my skin, I reflected on the past year. In a few months, the love of my life would become my wife. And if we stuck to our game plan, within the next couple of years, we'd welcome yet another bundle of joy into our lives. Five children, that was what we had our hearts set on. And I was more than willing to fork over any amount of money necessary in order for us to have the family we both wanted.

"I love you, you know that?" I asked.

Ellie's eyes looked up into my own. "I know. I love you, too. But, let's be quiet."

I lowered my voice to a whisper. "Why?"

She pointed. "April's falling asleep on you."

My heart warmed at the idea, and I walked over to the rocker by the window. I eased myself down, and Ellie propped a pillow up underneath my arm, and together we stared down at our child's sleeping face. Her lips softly pouted. Her eyes were tightly closed. She had a head full of dark hair like my own and her mother's little button nose. But, she definitely had my wide mouth and jawline.

"Poor girl's gonna have a Cheshire cat smile," I murmured.

Ellie swatted at me. "She's going to have your big smile, and I love that. I love your smile, and I love that she has it."

I chuckled. "I know you were worried about this pregnancy from front to back—"

"I mean, the doctor told us I only had four retrievable eggs during that hysterectomy. The odds were kind of stacked against us."

I kissed April's forehead. "Well, then let's thank our stars that we have a daughter willing to punch those odds in the face."

"Which reminds me, I do want to teach our children how to fight."

I looked over at her. "Oh?"

She nodded. "I don't want our kids to be pushovers. I don't want them starting fights, but I want them to feel confident enough in themselves to take up a fight on their own behalf if they feel it's necessary. If that makes sense."

I grinned. "If April's as feisty as her mother, I have no doubt that she won't have an issue with that."

A knock came at the door before Sadie's voice sounded. "Anybody home?"

Ellie came to life as she rushed over to the door. I heard her shushing people before ushering them in, and one by one, our family filled the room. Sadie and Will walked in with balloons. Willow and Bryce came in with pale-pink roses. Luna and Bart walked in with my two brothers, Wyatt and Boone, and together they hauled more present bags than I'd ever seen at once in my lifetime.

"What in the world?" I asked.

Sadie came up and whispered. "Can I see her sweet face? Oh, my goodness. Ellie, she looks just like you."

"That's what I said."

Will came over and patted my shoulder. "That's a good look for you, old man."

I chuckled. "Thanks. I think it's a pretty good look, too."

Willow dipped down in front of me. "Awww, she's a drooler. Anyone got a rag?"

Ellie tossed over my shirt. "That's already got spit up on it. You can use it."

Bryce smirked. "Baptism by fire, I hear."

I shrugged. "It's not that bad."

Ellie nodded. "He's had some preparation work before this. Micah can be pretty high maintenance sometimes."

I looked up. "Hey, hey, hey. If a man wants to do his hair in the bathroom a certain way, he has that right."

Ellie rolled her eyes. "Like I said, Ryan's made Micah high maintenance."

Bart pulled up a chair. "Want me to look through these packages and see if there's stuff you guys can use right now? I didn't see a go-bag or anything anywhere."

Ellie stared hard at me. "Yeah, because someone forgot to grab it from the guesthouse."

I shrugged. "Hey, I'm only capable of so much."

Bart grinned. "Well, Luna went on a crazy shopping spree, so I'm sure there's more than enough to help you guys out in here."

Luna swatted at him. "At least let Ellie open them."

Bart held up his hands. "Fine, fine. Just trying to help."

Ellie kissed his cheek softly. "And I thank you for it. Here, just hand them to me, and I'll open them all up."

As we ogled over the stuffed animals and the clothes and the sheer amount of diapers and wipes, I saw a familiar face peek into the room. Leslie's husband peered inside, so I waved him on in.

"You guys, this is Leslie's husband. You know, the woman who was our surrogate. Come on in, we're just opening some gifts."

He sheepishly stepped inside. "I know this isn't really protocol, but I wanted to stick my head in and make sure everything was okay? Leslie's getting a bit anxious."

I nodded. "It's totally okay. Would she like to see April?"

He shook his head. "My word will be enough. Do you guys need anything? She's pumping right now, but it takes a couple of days for the milk to really kick in."

Ellie walked over to the man. "You tell Leslie that we are perfect. April is healthy, all is good, and the hospital is supplying us with the milk we need while we're here. So, tell her to take some breaths and not to worry, because everything is all good on this end."

I blinked. "Are you sure she doesn't want to see the baby? Because I don't have an issue with it."

Ellie shook her head. "Neither do I."

Her husband smiled softly. "I'll pass the word on, but I think just knowing she's happy and healthy will be enough."

Ellie put her hand on the man's shoulder. "And if she struggles with her supply this time around, please tell her not to worry about it. We're already hooked up with a milk bank, so if all else fails, we've got that."

I nodded. "Yes, please tell her not to worry. You guys have already given us so much, I don't want her feeling as if she didn't do everything necessary. Because she's done more than enough."

Her husband smiled. "I'll definitely pass along that information, thank you."

Bryce piped up from the corner of the room. "I'm ordering barbecue. Y'all hungry?"

A sea of heads nodded before Ellie turned to Leslie's husband. "You think she's up for eating anything?"

He waved his hand in the air. "No, no, no. You guys are fine. Enjoy your family time, okay?"

I chuckled. "You two are as much a part of our family now as ever. So, if you think she could go for a barbecue plate and some cornbread, now's the time to speak up."

He paused. "You guys ordering from that place that does the pie, too?"

Bryce smiled. "Oh, yeah. That's where we always order from."

Ellie squeezed his shoulder. "Just tell Bryce what you and your wife want and come back by in around forty minutes or so. It should be here by then."

I shrugged. "Or stay and hang out. I don't care."

Ellie nodded. "Yep! That, too."

I saw Sadie out of the corner of my eye, snapping pictures with her camera. I heard the shutter clicking a million miles a second as she zoomed in on April's face and got much too close to mine. I let her do her thing, though, especially since it was out of the goodness of her heart.

And as I leaned in to kiss April's forehead, a familiar voice sounded in the room.

"She hewe?" Micah asked.

The crowd parted, and Mrs. Weatherford stepped through the door holding the hands of the twins. Micah stopped just in front of them, eyeing the small baby in my arms. But, he didn't go any farther until Ellie beckoned with her fingertip to come closer.

And when he saw his baby sister's face for the first time,

he leaned in to kiss her forehead. "Love oo, sister," he whispered.

I had to blink back tears as he climbed into my lap. Micah tucked his head underneath my chin as I cradled April in my other arm. He settled his hand on top of her leg, almost as if he were protecting her. Sadie continued with the pictures as quick as lightning while Ellie wiped away tears off in the corner. I wrapped my arm around Micah and held him close before I kissed the top of his head. And as I cradled my small family in my arms, I knew I couldn't have asked for a more perfect moment. Or a more perfect family.

"I love you, Micah," I whispered.

He giggled. "Love oo, too, Dah."

The entire room gasped as I pulled back, and my eyes immediately shot up to Ellie's. She cupped her hands over her mouth in utter shock before I looked back down at Micah, and I found his beautiful brown eyes staring widely up at me.

"No good?" he asked.

I smiled fondly down at him. "Very good. That's very good, Micah. You're more than welcome to call me that."

And his smile melted my fucking heart into a puddle of beautiful helplessness.

"My God, I love you so much," Ellie whispered.

She pressed a heated kiss against the top of my head before I tilted back. I gazed into her eyes from an upside-down position before she placed her lips against mine. Micah snuggled against me just as April started moving around, yawning and grunting and puckering her lips.

Ellie giggled. "Looks like someone's hungry again."

"I feed hew?" Micah asked.

I pointed to the bottle. "It's right there. Just hold it up to her lips, and I'll cradle her like this."

Sadie continued taking pictures as Ellie helped me to prop up April's head. She talked Micah through how to properly feed his little sister, and I lost myself in my own little world. The smell of barbecue quickly filled the air, but I didn't care. Bryce divvied out food and personally delivered an order to Leslie's room, but I didn't pay it any mind. The only thing that held my focus was my beautiful, wonderful family.

And as I thought about our upcoming wedding, the dream home we had started construction on, and our plans for more children, only one thought crossed my mind.

I finally found exactly what I want.

All it took was a beautiful single mother looking for a fresh start to completely turn my life around.

Follow Bella and Wyatt's journey to their HEA in
Cowboy's Innocent Assistant

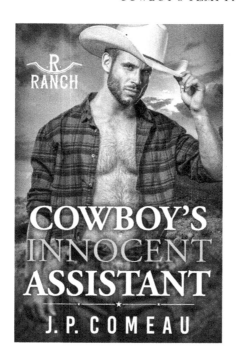

Made in the USA
Coppell, TX
01 August 2022

80746060R00125